THE SPONSOR

K. Kimuyu is a writer based in Nairobi, where he is currently working on his first poetry collection. *Lust Love & Longing* and his third novel. *Kesho & Malkia*. When he is not whacking away at the keyboard, you can find him taking long walks, or stopping to buy anything consumable by the roadside.

THE SPONSOR

K. Kimuyu

Editor: Michelle Korir

Cover design: Stephen Njogu

Author's website: www.kisauti.com

A copy of this book can be found at the Kenya National Library.

ISBN 978-9914-40-418-0

To purchase this book, write to

talk@kisauti.com

The city has a style, and the people wear it like the latest fashion.

- Nairobi

1.

The Family

Mzee Ajabu did not know when his family fell apart. It was not one thing; it was many little things. He could not even tell you the tipping point. But it was on his 67th birthday.

He came home as usual. He did not expect a party—he had been with his family for over 20 years now, and in none of those years had they celebrated his birthday. He expected the usual. A hot meal prepared by his wife, a shower, and hopefully, good sleep.

But something was different this birthday. His youngest child, Olivia, who had just cleared high school, was pregnant, and she wanted to be in his good books before she broke the news to him.

She loved her dad, despite whispers from her big sister, Wairimu, of him stepping out on their mom. She claimed to have seen him not once in town—arm in arm with young college girls.

Their sibling rivalry would not allow Olivia to take anything she said seriously. She wanted to show her big sister that she was superior to her. She had already taught Wairimu how to get pregnant, and soon, she would teach her how to get a husband.

Olivia had gone with her brother, Fred, to the supermarket, and they had bought cake, ribbons, and balloons, then gotten back to decorate their living room. There was no hurry; Mzee Ajabu usually came home late in the night, and tonight was no different.

Fred alerted them when he heard the sound of their father's Range Rover.

"Switch off the lights! He's here, he's here," he said, giddy with excitement.

They broke into song when he walked through the door, staggering because he had taken three fingers of Jack Daniel's at Muthaiga Country Club. But not even that could dampen their spirits.

Happy birthday to you,
Happy birthday to you…

They sang merrily, startling him as he closed the door behind him, and he realized pleasantly that tonight he would have to break his tradition.

Mrs. Ajabu joined in from the kitchen, carrying the cake, which had three candles sticking out of it.

Happy birthday dear Dad,
Happy birthday to you.

They sang some more as Mzee Ajabu huffed and puffed on the candles. His wife's face almost curled into a smile when he started breathing heavily.

"Breathe, Dad. We don't want death at a birthday," Fred said, and everyone giggled.

"What wish did you make, Dad?" Olivia asked cheerfully after he had blown them out.

"A happy and united family," Mzee Ajabu said proudly.

Just then, the lock on the door turned, Wairimu entered, and the mood changed. She was in a short dark thing that she called a dress, revealing most parts of her thighs, arms, and dipping cleavage. Her mother had long gotten tired of shouting at her, and her father had long gotten tired of telling her mother to talk to her.

She started walking towards her bedroom, and without notice, Mzee Ajabu grabbed her wrist. "Where are you coming from at this hour, Wairimu?" he asked, anger having replaced the pride and joy on his face. "I asked you a question, young lady."

Wairimu stared at him as if he was a brick wall.

"You're going to start working from tomorrow, and I no longer want to see you dressing like a prostitute," Mzee Ajabu barked, his hand digging into her wrist.

"You mean like the prostitutes you're cheating on Mom with?"

The words seemed to have sobered Mzee Ajabu. He got up and, with lightning speed, slapped her twice. She wrenched free and ran to her bedroom, sobbing. Nobody talked after that. They all disappeared into their rooms, except for Mrs. Ajabu, who sat beside her husband with a plate of hot food as she had always done.

2.

Mrs. Ajabu

MRS. AJABU SAT on the edge of their king-size bed, drinking wine from a large wine glass as Mzee Ajabu snored like a wild boar beside her. She knew what it meant to be the woman behind a successful man. She looked at his face and fought the urge to take a pillow and smother him till life left his body.

She took a swig from her wine glass, trying to wash from her mouth the taste of all those years she had endured him. She remembered the days when they were young, living in a shack made of timber and *mabati*. The days when Mzee Ajabu would come home drunk as a sponge and vomit all over the floor before pissing his pants, and she would be the one cleaning up after him in silence.

That was before the money came and the infidelities followed just as quickly, and she was the one staying behind to hold together the family even when it was slipping through her fingers like sand.

She was the one turning a blind eye and submitting to him, mind, body, and soul, even when her heart ached from his sins. She had thought of leaving but to where? To build another man and end up in the same shoes?

She took another swig and stared into the distance. Of course, sticking to the marriage had its benefits. They had built a family with two beautiful daughters and a handsome son, but she feared for the people they would turn out to be because of the mother she had been to them.

She moved her buttocks from left to right on the bed to get comfortable and wondered what they thought of her as a mother.

She was not on the best of terms with either of her daughters, Wairimu especially. She had beaten her up not once because of her insolence. A hint of a smile touched her face when she thought of her son, Fred. He was her lighthouse, the one who would save her.

She drank her wine and gazed at her husband. He was sleeping so that his big belly faced the ceiling. Maybe she could burst it with a needle, like she would a balloon. A smile curled on her face at the thought.

She looked at him and felt silly that she had once contemplated leaving him and taking nothing with her. If she ever left, she would take everything from him. The woman behind a successful man deserved nothing short of his success, she decided while emptying her glass.

3.

Wairimu

Wairimu woke up at 6:00 am, holding her brown teddy bear. Her cheeks were swollen to the point where she struggled to open her eyes, and her entire head rang like a siren. She had underestimated the strength of her father's fat, calloused hands, she realized, letting go of the teddy bear and getting out of bed. She picked a pair of Mara Moja tablets from her bedside stand and downed them with the water in the bottle beside them.

Wairimu had just finished campus with a Project Management degree. She did not want to do the course, but it was what her father had wanted, and so she had given it to him. She did not want to work in his advertising agency either. She wanted to be an activist, spearheading women's rights across the globe.

She went to the bathroom, turned the faucet to cold, and allowed the water to run on her face like needles of ice. She got back to her room feeling a bit refreshed.

She sat on her bed and cuddled her teddy bear. She had gotten it as a gift for herself after she turned 18. It had a recorder that connected to her phone wirelessly, and she sometimes used it to eavesdrop on her parents.

She got up and made her bed, which was in the far corner of the room. In the other corner were a laundry basket and a wardrobe with well-arranged clothes. At the window was a small desk stacked with books.

Chimamanda and Chinua Achebe were open on her desk. Further to the edge of the desk were other books—arranged so that you could only see their spines. There were: *The 48 Laws of Power*, *The Alchemist*, *War and Peace*, and *The Color Purple*. She sat down on her desk and closed Chimamanda's *Purple Hibiscus* with a bookmark, then turned the page on Chinua Achebe's *No Longer at Ease*.

Her stomach groaned, and she lifted her head from Chinua Achebe and glanced at her phone to check the time. The clock read 8:00 am. She knew her mother woke up at 9:00 am and her father at 10:00 am. She had less than an hour to eat, prepare, and leave.

She walked down the stairs and went to the kitchen to make her breakfast. Even with their big house, they did not have permanent domestic help. The house-helps usually came on weekends to do laundry and clean the house; otherwise, they were on their own.

She found Olivia in the kitchen.

"I'm craving sausages," she said.

She had been craving things of late, Wairimu noticed. *Is she pregnant? With that giant stick up her ass? She can't be*, she thought and giggled to herself.

"What's funny?" Olivia asked.

"Don't mind me. You know I'm crazy," Wairimu said and giggled again.

She went to the dining table and quickly gobbled up her plate of baked beans and glass of mango juice before her father could sniff her out.

Mzee Ajabu had wanted her to report to work today, but she had other plans. There was a women's rights demonstration that was happening in the city center, dubbed, *My Dress, My Choice*, and she was very much going to be at the forefront of it.

4.

Mzee Ajabu

MZEE AJABU WOKE up at 10:00 am with a feeling of gratitude. He looked at his wife's side of the bed. She had already woken up and ironed his clothes, and she was in the kitchen preparing his breakfast. He had married well, he thought.

His kids were okay. They had not made him as proud as he would have wanted, but they had not embarrassed him either. His youngest daughter was a sweethcart, his son did not indulge in drugs or hang out with crooks, and his eldest had cleared college without shaming him with pregnancies. It was only now that she was acting up, and he would rectify that promptly.

He got out of bed, entered the bathroom of their master bedroom, took a shower, and brushed his teeth after. He had long stopped going to work at the crack of dawn—age was catching up to him, and besides, his business was now a standing giant. He wore the pinstripe suit that his wife had laid out and went to the dining table.

His breakfast was waiting for him on the table. It was served heavy, the way he preferred it. He could not remember when it was not like this. Waking up to clean, ironed clothes and hot food. He drank his tea, sipping it so that he made slurping sounds, and ate his mashed potatoes and beef stew followed by yams, which he downed with a second cup of tea.

His wife sat two paces from him with a wrapper on her head and a *leso* fastened around her waist, watching the news on TV. He looked at her, and he saw the girl he had married many years ago.

"What is Fred doing with himself lately?" he groaned in between the sounds of his teeth digging into his food.

It always baffled Mrs. Ajabu how he asked questions about his kids as if he did not live with them under the same roof.

"His graduation is coming up. We're going to need to throw a small party for him." She did not feel the need to tell her husband that Fred had dropped out of school almost a year ago now to pursue music, even though he was still giving her money for his fees.

"A party?" His face contorted into a frown. "That will cost us."

They were not doing any major projects, yet he was complaining about money. She wondered what he was doing with his CEO salary, but she did not ask.

"Let me think about it," Mzee Ajabu said as she poured a third cup of tea for him. "Where is Wairimu?" he asked.

"She should be in her room," Mrs. Ajabu replied.

"Wairimu!" he called. Before he could call again, his Kabambe beeped.

He had two phones, a Samsung Note and a Kabambe. Whenever his Samsung rang, it was work. He screamed into it about incompetent employees and good-for-nothing managers.

But whenever his Kabambe rang, he got up, excused himself, and whispered in the corridor, bedroom, or balcony.

He looked at his Kabambe's screen, and his face gleamed. He got up, and Mrs. Ajabu helped him with his coat. "It's work. We will talk about this further in the evening."

"The groceries are almost finished," Mrs. Ajabu sang. She knew when her husband was lying, and she used it as an opportunity to fleece him.

"I will send you the money," he said while turning the doorknob.

He got to the parking lot and found his driver waiting for him. He had married well, he thought as his driver opened the back-left door of his Range Rover for him, and his watchman saluted as he was driven out of his Runda home.

5.

The Prodigal Son

FRED WOKE UP at noon. He thought of getting out of bed and opening his curtains but then decided he did not need the light hurting his eyes. He reached for his phone from his bedside table; as he did, his ashtray and an empty bottle of Jack Daniel's fell to the floor. He loaded an adult website, reached for his Vaseline, and moved his hands beneath his blanket.

There was a knock on his door as his hand moved up and down underneath the blanket.

"Fred, Fred, are you awake?"

"I'm busy, Mom."

"Are you coming to eat breakfast?"

"I'm coming."

He got out of bed with a patch of liquid around the groin area of his boxers. He looked at the pile of empty bottles of Jack Daniel's and pizza boxes in one corner of his room, then moved his gaze to the pile of clothes in the other corner. He walked towards the pile of clothes and pulled out trousers and a t-shirt.

After putting on the clothes, he picked up his phone and stood for a minute to look at the piano his mother had bought him after he dropped out of college. It stood sentry in the middle of his bedroom, collecting dust and tormenting him. He had put it there as a reminder that he needed to practice his music, but God knew he had not touched it in months.

The thought of sitting at it and playing made him flee his bedroom. He went down the stairs and sat at the dining table with his mom. There was a carton of mango juice, sausages, bread, and the yams his father had left. He poured himself a glass of juice, put four sausages on a plate, and started buttering four slices of bread.

"How is music practice coming along?" his mother asked.

"It's going great, Mom, but I told you I need classes to get better," Fred said, annoyed. He sipped his juice, broke a sausage in half, and threw it into his mouth.

"You know your father won't hear any of that. He knows you're doing finance. He expects you to succeed him."

"Screw Dad," he said, chewing his bread and sipping his mango juice.

"I have gotten a hold of some cash." She picked up her phone from the table. "There, I have sent you 50,000 bob. Go and pay for the classes you're stressed about. I will give you the rest next month."

Fred opened his phone, and the video on the adult website started playing. Mrs. Ajabu pretended to be distracted by her phone. He then thumbed the message with the money transfer and grinned. He knew the first thing he would do with the money, and it wasn't paying fees for music classes.

6.

Olivia

OLIVIA CALCULATED WHILE she listened to her mother and her brother from the kitchen. She had planned to break the news to her dad first, but after the hot slaps he had landed on Wairimu's stupid face, she had reconsidered and decided her mother would be the best one to tell, and then *she* could ease their dad into it.

She listened to their conversation in surprise. It was no secret that their mother loved Fred more than anyone else in that house, but she did not think it was to the extent of giving him everything he wanted. Now she wished she had that kind of favor, but she knew she didn't.

She had woken up early, washed the dishes, made breakfast, and cleaned their gigantic living room. Her mother had raised an eyebrow. It wasn't that Olivia wasn't hard-working, but Mrs. Ajabu knew her daughter. She was not the type to volunteer to do something when she didn't have to.

After Fred left—in too much of a hurry, if she was asked—Olivia tied her flowing hair into a bun and walked into the living room. She found her mother plopped on the sofa, twisting her hair into *matuta* while watching Telemundo.

"Mom, I need to talk to you," she said, her fingers interlocked in front of her purple *dera* and her eyes firmly on the floor.

Mrs. Ajabu switched off the TV. "About what?" she asked.

Olivia took a seat opposite her mother. Her hips filled up the entire couch. She was built like a pear: her chest was small, her waist tiny, and her hips wide. She sat on the edge of it, ready to bolt in case her mom flew into a rage.

"Something I have been meaning to tell you…"

"You're pregnant, aren't you?" Mrs. Ajabu said while fastening her wig on top of her *matuta*.

Olivia's gaze remained on the floor.

"You grow a bit of hips and the first thing you do is spread your legs wide for men? Who is he?"

"He works in the bank. We…we met in the supermarket," Olivia stammered.

"I send you shopping and you invite men to your bed?"

She remained silent.

"What's his name?"

"Larry."

"Does he know?"

"Yes."

"And?"

"He does not want anything to do with it." She broke into an inaudible sob, and her bun came undone, letting her hair fall on her face.

"Do you want to keep it?"

"I don't know," she said, tucking her hair behind her ears.

"How far along are you?"

"About two months," she said as she wore her hairband on her wrist.

"You're in the first trimester; it's not even a baby yet."

Olivia looked at her mother blankly and fiddled with her hairband.

"Go and get ready. It's time we paid our family doctor a visit," Mrs. Ajabu said expansively.

7.

Fred

THE SUN WAS up in the sky. Fred jumped over a puddle of sewer water and almost knocked down an old woman on the roadside as he avoided a speeding motorbike.

He wiped the sweat from his brow as he walked away from the tall buildings that housed corporate offices in Westlands, and into a gated community with pine trees lining the roads, and corrugated iron sheets sitting on the houses' heads.

Fred stopped at a black iron-bar gate. He rang the bell twice and peeked through the bars. There was a Jeep parked outside the house, and a sprinkler made sounds as it watered the manicured lawn. After what felt like half an hour, a guard wearing blue overalls appeared at the gate.

"*Unataka nini?*" he asked.

"My name is Fred. I'm here to see Jack."

The guard disappeared into his booth. Fred looked up and saw the surveillance camera staring at him, and he looked at his shoes.

Five minutes passed before the gate was opened. It was quite a distance to the main house. He busied himself with the sounds of the sprinkler as he walked up the long driveway. He got to the door and pressed the doorbell.

The main door was made of iron and behind it was another door made of wood. An eye peeped out through the wooden door, and out stepped the short, slender man who went by the name Jack.

"Come in," he said after opening the iron door.

It took a second for Fred's eyes to adjust to the darkness inside. It was a large, empty room with dark, heavy curtains—nothing like what it looked like on the outside. There was a weight bench in one corner and an AK-47 leaning against the wall in the other corner. In the middle of the room was a small TV playing the news and a tattered couch, beside which was a table with all sorts of powders and bottles of Tusker.

"Are you here for the usual?" Jack asked.

"Yeah."

"Have a seat."

Fred hesitated. On the couch was seated a tall man in a black vest and combat shorts. He had dreadlocks and a brown-colored goatee. He was watching the breaking news of the *My Dress, My Choice* demonstration happening in Nairobi's city center and taking a swig from a bottle of Tusker.

"Don't worry about him. That's my buddy, Jamuel. All he does is sit on my couch and drink all my beer."

Fred went back to the table where Jack was preparing his package. "Instead of the usual roll, give me three rolls of weed today."

"Uh, Jamuel, Freddie boy has money today." Jack smiled, and a golden tooth glinted in the dim light. Jamuel had left the couch and was now lifting weights on the weight bench.

"If you've got dough, I can hook you up with something better than weed. Something that will take you straight to heaven," Jack chirped.

"Just give me the weed that I'm used to."

"Look, because you're a frequent customer, I'll give you a bit of powder. Draw it into a line with a piece of paper like this"—Jack poured some powder on the table and lined it up with a paper—"and give it a sniff." He blocked the left side of his nose and snorted it with his right nostril and jumped up. "Whoa! Feels damn near better than my girlfriend."

"Guess it wouldn't hurt to try," Fred said, warming up to the idea.

"Let me put my money where my mouth is, my friend." Jack put a hand on Fred's shoulder. "If it doesn't take you to another world, come and ask me for a lifetime supply of weed." Jack shook his head vigorously, as if trying to get a grip of his senses. "Jamuel, get the door for Freddie boy," he said finally.

Jamuel got up from the weight bench and walked past Fred. As he opened the door, Fred noticed the Glock that was tucked into his trousers' waistband. He got out of the house, his eyes hurting from adjusting to the sun blaring in the sky. He heard the sound of the sprinkler and felt relief and then excitement to try the new product.

8.

The Demo

THE GROUP OF skimpily dressed women walked through the roads of Nairobi's city center with their banners, chanting, "My dress, my choice." At the back of the group were the somewhat modestly dressed—in thigh-length miniskirts and crop-tops with plunging necklines. In the middle were the ones in swimsuits, and at the front, most wore small fabrics and strings that covered their private parts, but their breasts were exposed for the world to see.

Wairimu was in a red bikini and black sandals in the front line with the eccentrics. She was in the front because she knew that was where the media would be. She lifted her banner and ran to one of the cameramen. "My dress, my choice," she chanted.

She lifted her top and flashed her breasts at the cameraman. That was certain to make it to prime-time TV, she decided. A smile curled on her face when she imagined her dad watching the news.

The women became rowdier as they approached Parliament, where the lawmakers were threatening to pass a draconian bill that would keep women from wearing their miniskirts. Some women stopped every now and then to dry-hump a street light pole or a tree.

They walked in their nakedness and high heels, cursing men and the world for failing to respect them enough, till they got to the gates of Parliament. Nobody could say where the rotten eggs, cabbages, and tomatoes had come from, but they were now being hurled at the guards manning the gates. "Let us in!" they shouted at one of the guards, who had egg on his face.

A gunshot was heard. Then smoke appeared. "Teargas!" someone screamed. Another gunshot was heard, and more smoke filled Parliament Road. The ladies screamed as they scattered. Some fell while trying to run in their high heels, but there was nowhere to run. Behind them was a police tank spraying water at tremendous speeds—water that could rip flesh from bone if it touched you.

Wairimu rubbed her eyes, still chanting, "My dress, my choice," with the little energy she had left. She was covered with the grime from the rotten eggs and tomatoes. "My dress, my choice," she chanted, not really seeing where she was going because the teargas had blinded her. "My dress, my choice," she mumbled, walked two steps, and hit hard, solid iron. It was a police patrol car. The next thing she felt was ice-cold handcuffs wrapping around her delicate wrists.

9.

Mzee Ajabu

WHILE HIS YOUNGEST daughter was preparing for her doctor's appointment, his son getting a bag of drugs, and his eldest daughter being arrested, Mzee Ajabu was lying naked in a queen-size bed in the suburbs of Lavington, being fed a bowl of grapes by Diana.

Diana was yellow-skinned, short, shapely, with long braids, and not older than 21. Mzee Ajabu loved the braids; they came in handy when he mounted her from behind. Diana put the bowl of grapes away and rubbed his chest hair. "We should go to Dubai for a week," she groaned.

Mzee Ajabu pretended not to have heard her. Her head was now resting on his chest so that Mzee Ajabu's left hand had enough room to cup her buttocks. Every time he did, she moved closer to him, almost as if she wanted to wear his skin like a piece of cloth. He loved it.

"Imagine the tall buildings, the sand dunes, the beach. It will be so relaxing," she added.

"I have a company to run and a family to go home to, my dear. I can't just up and go to Dubai without notice."

"Imagine having sex at the Burj Khalifa?"

Mzee Ajabu stared at the marbled white ceiling with a fan doing the rounds and entertained the idea.

"You know, there are some sex moves I have reserved for Dubai."

They both laughed. He had met her after she had come straight from the village and joined Nairobi University to pursue a degree in anthropology—a course she hated. He had been so enthralled by her youth and beauty that he had paid her tuition in a top private university where she could study Public Relations, gotten her an apartment in Lavington, and put her on a very healthy allowance, and now she was spoiled rotten.

"Let me think about it," he said finally as they got out of bed and went to the bathroom.

Diana turned the faucet of the bathtub to warm water, and when Mzee Ajabu got in, she started lathering him with soap. It was a chore she didn't enjoy, but it was a small price to pay for what he did for her, she knew. "You missed a spot," Mzee Ajabu said, lifting his armpits.

After rinsing, toweling, oiling, and massaging him, she clothed him, and they headed to the dining table.

Her full-time house-help fixed Diana a plate of bacon, eggs, and baked beans with a cup of green tea. She started fixing Mzee Ajabu a plate of yams and *turungi*, but he stopped her.

"I won't eat today," he said.

"You're sure you don't want anything?" Diana asked while spooning beans into her mouth.

"If I eat one more thing, I won't be able to walk."

"Fix him a plate just in case he changes his mind," Diana

asked her house-help.

Mzee Ajabu kissed her on the lips, considering the Dubai vacation. It wasn't a bad idea. Not at all. Being away from his company and his family would help him blow off steam, and he would be the better for it, he decided.

"I will tell my operations team to plan for a week's vacation in the most luxurious hotel in Dubai," he said as Diana buttoned up his coat.

"OMG! You're the best," she sang, hugging and smooching him all over the face. "We will have so much fun, you'll see."

"Get ready. We leave in the evening," Mzee Ajabu said as she walked him to the door, and he dissolved into his corporate life.

10.

Ajabu Digital

MZEE AJABU HAD built a multi-billion-shilling company. It occupied four floors in the Mirage Tower in Westlands, Nairobi and boasted over 1,000 employees across the country. Besides being the pioneer of digital advertising at a time when nobody saw its benefit, Mzee Ajabu had another secret: he took on as many clients as he could while paying his employees peanuts and working them till late into the night.

Ajabu Digital had risen like cream to the top. The cash flow deficit was immense and the turnover staggering. Oftentimes, an employee would burst into tears at their desk and leave, never to be seen again.

But what were cash flow problems when they could be buffered with loans, and what were employees but bodies that could be replaced at a moment's notice by the bevy of jobless youths waiting in their Human Resource careers inbox?

Mzee Ajabu sat in his office, fiddling with his pen, a myriad of thoughts racing through his mind.

It was a big office with a small boardroom at the center, where most status meetings took place with the company's executives. On the left side of the office was a door that led to a fully furnished apartment, complete with a kitchen and bedroom.

He opened the latest file in his in-tray. It was from his Chief Financial Officer. He did not like the numbers on the first page. The problem with a big company was that it demanded too much working capital upfront. Clients never paid on time and, well, rent needed to be paid, a broken window fixed, employees' salaries paid. All these things needed money, and that was how Ajabu Digital found itself with cash flow problems.

Mzee Ajabu fiddled with his pen and opened the next page. They had just acquired Mambo Tele—the biggest maize flour company in the country—on a 60-day payment policy. A smile touched his face, but it disappeared just as quickly when he turned to the last page.

Some clients had not paid them for over a year. He picked up his phone and dialed his CFO. "Let's try to close these debts running for over a year this month," he said and hung up. The credit department was already stretched thin, but it could be stretched further, he decided.

He opened the next file. It was from his Chief Operating Officer. They were documents that would see the company expand into Uganda and Rwanda. He closed the file momentarily and looked at his golden Bell & Ross limited edition watch. It was striking noon, and his daughter, Wairimu, was nowhere to be seen.

His heart had been feeling heavy lately. He was aging quickly, and he did not have a sure successor. After his company was incorporated, he had made it so that the shareholding was spread equally between him and his children. But he was now feeling that none of them were ready.

He closed his eyes for a second and hoped his eldest daughter would get out of her stupor. If Fred became the CEO, he wanted Wairimu to be the COO, and Olivia? Well, his flower would be the Chief Human Resource Officer.

He had planned it all in his head, down to a T. He would retire at 70 and move to his beach house in Mombasa, and his work would be reduced to overseeing.

He finished signing the documents that would see them expand to Uganda and Rwanda, leaned back in his chair, and contemplated calling Wairimu. He then contemplated calling his wife. He picked up his phone and dialed his pilot's number. He had plans to be in Dubai.

11.

Inmate

THE IRON BARS clinked shut, and Wairimu was left inside the cell, shivering in her bikini and sandals. She had thought she was alone until she heard heavy breathing behind her. She turned around to find two women standing in front of her and another one hunched in the corner in a fetal position.

The first one was short and fat with crooked yellow teeth and a face that looked as if it had been smashed in with an axe. A rhino came to mind every time Wairimu looked at her—not directly, but while half-staring at the floor. Her t-shirt and trouser were baggy, but they looked small on her.

The other one was chewing her gum loudly. She was tall and thin, with a flimsy dress that cut above her thighs. She had drawn her eyebrows so that she looked like she was surprised the entire time. She could do with one or two YouTube makeup tutorials, Wairimu thought. The name her father had called her the previous night came to mind every time she glanced at her.

The one in the corner had no shoes, and her dress was torn to shreds. Her face was caked with drying blood—she looked as if she had just been mauled by a lion. Wairimu shuddered as she saw her fate flash before her eyes. She had not decided her next move when Madam Rhino came close to her.

"Wewe umefanya nini ndio uletwe hapa?"

"Hakuna," she said with a trembling voice.

"Hawa ni wale hutuibia mabwana," Surprised Eyebrows said, smacking her mouth as she chewed her gum.

"Hata ule kwa corner ni mwizi wa mabwana kama wewe," Madam Rhino added.

"Hapana, sikuiba bwana," Wairimu said, wanting to burst into tears and reflexively covering her face as Madam Rhino charged towards her. But before she could get a hold of her, the iron bars clinked open, and her name was called.

"Inaonekana Mungu wako halali," a fat female police officer said as they walked to the reception desk where her dad's driver was waiting.

"I have been sent to pick you up by your dad," the driver said to Wairimu.

"She needs to fill the papers," the fat female officer interrupted.

"She doesn't need to fill anything. She is Mzee Ajabu's daughter. Delete her mugshots and fingerprints from the database," a policeman standing next to the driver barked.

It was getting dark when Wairimu entered her dad's Range Rover with the driver's coat around her shoulders. She remembered calling her mom with the single call she was given and telling her what had happened. Mrs. Ajabu had not been in the mood to cover for her, in any case, her husband already knew his daughter was rotten.

She had called Mzee Ajabu, and he had placed a call to his

driver and another one to the officer commanding the police division. Within minutes, Wairimu was getting out of her cell. She now sat at the back of her dad's car, her heart racing, and she realized that she was more fearful and anxious inside the car than she had been in the cell.

12.

Olivia

OLIVIA'S PULSE STARTED racing the moment she entered the small clinic with her mother. There were images of fetuses on the wall that reminded her of her biology classes in high school. She stopped for a second and stared at one—the same thing was growing inside her body, and in a few minutes, it would be no more, she thought.

"It's just a bunch of cells you're getting rid of; no bigger than an eyebrow," Mrs. Ajabu said, as if she had heard her train of thought.

Her mother's words did not ease things; they just quickened the speed of her pulse. Mrs. Ajabu left her at the waiting area and went to fill her papers at the reception desk. Olivia picked an old medical magazine from the coffee table and started flipping through the pages. She stopped at an article titled, "Termination of Pregnancy."

There were two common methods to terminate a pregnancy,

or as her mother put it, to get rid of cells. The first one involved taking pills that stopped the hormones in charge of nourishing the baby and another pill that induced cramping. The other one included sharp needles and a suction pump. Olivia gasped with trepidation as if seeing her fate.

Mrs. Ajabu hobbled back to the waiting area. "Don't look at that," she barked, snatching the magazine from her daughter's hands. Olivia did not see her mother coming nor hear what she had said because of the ringing in her head. She only felt the magazine fly off her hands. She did not even hear the nurse calling her name; it was her mother who nudged her. "Get up," she said while grabbing her hand. "They are ready for us."

Their family doctor was a middle-aged man who went by the name Dr. Onyango. Besides being employed by Nairobi Hospital, he had opened his own private practice, where he earned extra income through underhanded procedures.

He now stood in front of Olivia and her mother in a white lab coat with red stains. His face sagged, making him look older than he was. He did not look anxious or calm, cheerful or sad— he had a face that looked like it had seen things that it shouldn't have. Olivia thought his face resembled death.

The first thing he did was explain the two procedures.

"The pill route will be harder on your body, so we will go the suction-pump way, which will be easier on you, understood?"

Olivia did not remember saying yes or no.

"I will put you on anesthesia. You will feel drowsy but when you wake up, it will all be over, and you can go back to your normal life."

She was directed to the changing room. She wore the loose-fitting clothes that were provided and headed to the surgery room with her pulse in her throat. She lay on the stiff bed in the middle of the room and stared at the bright fluorescent

lights. A gas mask was placed over her nose, and her pulse started receding as something cold opened up her vagina, and she
faded away into another world.

This world did not have a doctor who resembled death
or a mother who snatched magazines from her hands. It had
blossoming flowers, birds singing, and people laughing joyfully.
She was having a picnic in the park with her husband, Larry, and
their son was playing with other kids, and every now and then, he
would come and kiss her on the forehead.

"I love you, Mom," he would say before running back to the
other kids.

Then the flowers started withering, the birds stopped singing, and the joyful laughter turned into screaming. She was in a
different world, one without anesthesia, and she could feel hot,
searing pain exploding in her stomach and between her thighs.
Someone was tearing open her cervix with a knife and stabbing
her son multiple times.

Olivia woke up with a screech. "Stop! Stop! Stop killing my
son!"

"Relax, Olivia. It's over," Dr. Onyango said, the look of
death on his face now heightened.

She looked at him with a pleading face. "Don't kill him, I
beg of you." The doctor stared at her blankly, and Olivia fell
back to her pillow softly and felt a big scar open up within her.

13.

Fred

FRED SAT SHIRTLESS on a chair on his balcony, lit the blunt he had bought, and watched the sun going down while listening to E-sir's "Nimefika" album on his phone, through his headphones. He took a long pull, blew a cloud of smoke into the air, and stared into the distance. His balcony had a beautiful view of trees and lights from the neighboring houses. He thought of entering his room and composing music in honor of the view but took another pull instead.

He took a final pull and crushed the remains of the blunt with his foot. His eyes were bloodshot, and he felt higher than a kite. He blew a cloud of smoke into the air and wondered how high he could get. His mind kept going back to the white powder that was sitting in his room.

"Draw it into a line with a piece of paper and give it a sniff...if it doesn't take you to another world, come and ask me for a lifetime supply of weed."

Fred stared into the distance. It had gotten dark now. He watched the lit-up houses for a while, and his high began to recede.

There was a foul smell around him, and it wasn't the weed. He sniffed his armpits and wrinkled his nose. Maybe he should jump in the shower, he thought. After rolling another joint, he decided while removing his headphones and getting up from his chair.

He opened the bag that was sitting on his bed and saw the weed and the powder. He hesitated momentarily and got a hold of the sealed transparent bag with the white powder. He lined a bit of it on his table with a piece of paper. He blocked his left nostril with his thumb, snorted it with his right nostril, and went back to the balcony thinking it had been a waste of his time. A smile touched his face when he thought about his lifetime supply of weed from Jack.

He put his headphones back on and stared into the distance as "Leo Ni Leo" filled his ears. Ten minutes had not passed when the balcony started spiraling in slow circular motions. Fred got up from his chair, worried, and took a hold of the balcony rails. They felt like cooked spaghetti underneath his grip. He looked at the trees and the houses in the distance—the trees were on fire, and the lights in the houses had turned into fireworks. He sat back on his chair and felt as if he had dived into the deep end of a pool.

His feet were off the ground, his heart was beating out of his chest, and his head was floating in the clouds. He was in a new world, he realized. In this world, he was seated next to his piano, composing melodious tunes that the world had never heard before, and he was being interviewed by all the major TV and radio stations.

Outside, fans were shouting his name. "Fred, I love you!"

A young girl with a shapely body threw her panties at him. Fred brushed it off and shrugged. He was used to it.

The next moment, he was in State House with the president of Kenya, about to be appointed as the tourism ambassador for the country. He was about to start traveling around the world to the sound of adoring fans. But just as he was about to shake the president's hand, something cold hit his face, and he woke up from his fantasy.

It was poop from a bird chirping on the balcony from the excitement of a new day. Fred wiped the poop off with his hand. He got up groggily and shooed the bird off, almost toppling over the balcony. He picked his phone and headphones from the floor, walked to his room, went to the stash of white powder that was left, and drew it into a line. He snorted it all and went back to being a pop star.

14.

Olivia

BOTH MOTHER AND daughter sat silently in the taxi on their way back home. Mrs. Ajabu was seated in the front seat, staring at the road unblinking, and Olivia was seated in the back looking pale. She leaned into her seat, opened her mouth, and a green, gooey substance spilled out. She did not bother moving. She sat motionless as her vomit flowed onto the seat and seeped into her clothes as the taxi maneuvered through Nairobi's traffic.

"Madam, your…" the driver started to speak.

"Don't worry about it. I'll pay you for the trouble," Mrs. Ajabu interrupted.

The taxi shook after hitting a pothole on the road, and Olivia moved on her seat the way an empty box without support would. Mrs. Ajabu glanced at the rear-view mirror and clenched her jaw. She had done what was necessary. Her daughter would thank her for it when she got older, she assured herself.

The taxi slowed down as it approached their home, and their watchman opened the gate. Mrs. Ajabu led the way, and her daughter dragged behind like a bag of rocks. They entered the house, and she fell with a plop on one of the sofas in their living room.

"Get up and go to your room. What will people say if they find you here?" Mrs. Ajabu barked. Olivia moved her feet from the floor to the sofa and got comfortable.

"I said go to your room!"

She lay on the sofa, unmoving, like a stone. Mrs. Ajabu tried to carry her, but she was now a woman, not the child she used to carry around with a *leso*. She wondered silently where Wairimu and Fred were and thought of seeking their help but decided against it. This needed to stay a secret between her and Olivia.

She placed the medication and the hospital documents on the table and went outside to look for their watchman.

Olivia was in a river of pain. She felt it more in her spirit than in her body. She remembered the knife being dragged through her womb and stirred on the sofa. "Don't kill my son, I beg of you," she mouthed, but she was too weak to be heard by anyone. "Don't kill my son, I beg of you," she mouthed again as darkness swallowed her.

15.

Wairimu

WAIRIMU WAS ANXIOUSLY waiting for the duel with her father. She had left her teddy bear in the sitting room. She tapped on the recording application on her phone and plugged in her earphones. "Go to your room," she heard her mother bark. She was sure her siblings were being cleared from the room. Any minute now, her mom would be banging on her door, and she would be face to face with her father.

It's how it always happened when she did something her parents did not approve of. Her mom would bang on her door relentlessly, and when she didn't open, she would get the spare key and drag her out. She would get to the living room to find her dad waiting with a belt. "I hate him," she mumbled while locking her door and using her reading chair to secure it further.

She stayed alert and listened, but all she heard were movements in the living room and the main door being banged. A moment later, she heard a faint voice saying, "Don't kill my son."

She rubbed her face and blinked twice, wondering if she was hallucinating. She removed her earphones, opened her bedroom door slightly, and heard it again, "Don't kill my son, I beg of you."

Wairimu rushed to their living room to find Olivia lying on the sofa in a fetal position, looking lifeless. On the table beside her were bottles of medicine and an envelope. She picked a bottle and read the label; it was a prescription to relieve pain. She picked another one; it was meant to ease cramping.

She put the bottle down and removed the document from the envelope. Immediately she read it, her knees got weak. She sat next to her sister and looked at her lying there like a block of meat, and she was overwhelmed with sorrow. *Why did I go to the protest? I could have saved her,* she thought. *This must be Dad's work,* she decided.

"Olivia, are you okay? Olivia. Olivia." She shook her, but she was unmoving except for the gentle up and down movements of her chest.

Wairimu got up, deciding to let her rest. She picked her teddy bear and went back to her room. She sat on her bed with her shoulders hunched and hugged the teddy bear. *As if stepping out on Mom isn't enough, now this?* she thought and burst into tears for her sister and for herself.

She felt defeated. Then she thought for a moment and realized that her father's power stemmed from having money and status. If all that was ripped away, he would be nothing. She decided that she would start working at her father's advertising agency, climb through the ranks, and then take everything that was dear to him. She sat up with a new look in her eyes—that of vengeance.

16.

Mrs. Ajabu

AFTER TUCKING IN Olivia and burning the medical documents, Mrs. Ajabu sat in the living room, feeling accomplished. She had just saved her daughter from motherhood and shame in one fell swoop. She switched the TV to Telemundo and looked at the screen without watching the show that was playing, before getting up and going to the kitchen.

It had two fridges; a big one and a smaller one. The big one was accessible to the entire family, and the other one was hers. She reached into her bra and came out with a small key. She opened her fridge and took out a fresh bottle of red wine. She poured herself a large glass, locked the fridge, and returned the key into her bra.

She sat on the sofa and took long swigs from the glass while staring at the TV without seeing the show. She emptied her glass, went to the kitchen, and came back with another full glass. She took big gulps and groaned, remembering the phone conversation she had had with her husband after tucking in Olivia.

She had asked him what he wanted to eat for supper, and he had told her he wouldn't make it because he was going on a business trip to Dubai for a week. "It was last-minute notice. We're thinking of opening another branch there," he had said before hanging up.

Mrs. Ajabu emptied the glass with another long swig. She sat on the sofa for a long while and stared at the TV without seeing it. She switched it off and went to the kitchen, then headed to their master bedroom with a fresh bottle of red wine. She sat on the edge of the bed, popped it open, and drank straight from the bottle, wondering if she should call Fred and tell him the plans she had for him.

She had no qualms with her son pursuing his music, but he needed to realize that he was destined for greater things than pressing a bunch of black and white blocks on a board. She wondered how she would entice him. She knew he liked smoking. She also knew he had dreams of grandeur. That was his Achilles' heel and her window to get to him, she decided.

Mrs. Ajabu emptied the bottle of red wine and stared at the bedroom wall for a long time. She thought of getting up, putting the empty bottle in the dustbin, and changing into her nightdress—then she collapsed on the bed with the bottle beside her and felt the room spinning and spinning before she passed out.

17.

Mzee Ajabu

Mzee Ajabu was in white sneakers, khaki trousers, and a blue polo shirt. He did not dress that way often, only once or twice a year when he went golfing with corporate honchos at Muthaiga Country Club to discuss business. But today was a special occasion. He wanted to impress Diana, show her that he could also be hip. Age, after all, was nothing but a number.

A dark BMW UberSELECT parked at Wilson Airport, and Diana stepped out. She was in sandals and a see-through purple dress. Her thick braids flowed as she approached Mzee Ajabu. She looked, in every sense, like a spoiled tycoon's daughter.

"I have really missed you," she said with a honey-glazed voice, as if they had not been together that very morning, and planted a soft kiss on his leathery skin.

Mzee Ajabu's face flushed with excitement. "Are you ready for Dubai?" he asked, grabbing her small waist and pulling her to him.

"I was born ready," she giggled as they entered his Gulfstream G550, fingers intertwined.

The Uber driver got Diana's humongous bags out of the boot. The air hostess made a signal to one of the baggage handlers, and he ran and dragged the bags into the Gulfstream.

They entered the cabin and sat together on the divan-style seat. Diana crossed her legs and her purple dress rolled up. Mzee Ajabu placed his fat, calloused hand on her yellow thigh, and she leaned into him and placed her head on his chest.

They sat cuddled as if they needed each other for oxygen as the air hostess served them sparkling wine, and the two Rolls Royce engines of the G550 roared as it left the hangar at Wilson Airport.

The nose of the huge bird faced the runway, and it started stretching its legs—slowly at first, and then galloping, and within seconds they were airborne: making toasts and giggling. *This is what wealth is all about,* Mzee Ajabu thought as they watched the sunset at an altitude of 40,000 feet.

18.

Withdrawal Symptoms

FRED WAS WOKEN up by a nightmare. A heavily built man had just tackled him to the floor, and there was a ringing in the back of his head. He couldn't remember how he got from his balcony chair to the hard, cold floor of his room. He felt nauseated. He lifted his head to go to the toilet and slammed back to the floor as though his body was a ton of bricks.

He finally managed to get up, and he staggered to the toilet and vomited. He washed his hands, rinsed his mouth, and went back to his bedroom. He sat on his bed, confused; his mouth was dry and his skin was itchy.

He had not eaten the whole day, yet he did not feel hungry. He looked outside; it was dark. He got under the covers and tried to get some sleep, but sleep would not come. He scratched his skin and tossed this way and that way. He needed another hit of the powder badly, he realized.

He got out of his bed and picked up the empty bag of powder. "Fuck. Who took my stash?" he barked while trying to sniff the empty bag. He dropped it on the floor and held his head in the palm of his hands. It felt as if it was on fire.

He got out of his room and went to the kitchen. He found Wairimu microwaving leftover food.

"Where is Mom?" he asked her.

"Don't know, don't care."

"What about Dad?"

Wairimu went quiet, her hatred for her dad overwhelming her. She took her food without looking at her brother and went to her room.

"Shit. Shit. What kind of a house is this that doesn't have Mara Moja?" Fred barked some more while opening one kitchen cabinet after the other. The kitchen floor was littered with flour, salt, sugar, and broken glasses when he left.

He lay on his bed with his eyes wide open for what felt like an hour before sleep took him. He did not sleep for long before the barking of dogs woke him up.

There were no dogs, nor barking, he realized after some time and got back on his pillow. Sleep took him momentarily before he was woken up by floods. He got out of bed and ran to his balcony. He gripped the rails of the balcony, breathing hard. He wiped the sweat from his brow with the back of his hand as he came to the realization that there were no floods.

The nausea was worse now, his skin was itchier than it had been, and he had a splitting migraine. He needed all of it to stop. He went back to his room, took his phone, and dialed Jack.

"Jack, I need some more of the powder," he panted into his phone when Jack picked.

"Freddie boy, that shit is magic, isn't it?"

"I need it now. Can you give me the same deal you gave me if I buy the same amount of weed?"

"No, Freddie boy, this time it's going to cost you."

"How much?"

"15K a bag, but because you're my boy, I will give it to you for 10K."

He did the math. He had bought the bag of weed for 5,000 and remained with 45,000 bob—money that he had planned to use to put a down payment on his music classes.

"That's too much," he said and kicked his table, hurting his foot. "Ouch!" he groaned.

"Suit yourself, Freddie boy," Jack said and hung up.

Fred pulled his hair. He tried to swallow his saliva, but he couldn't. His throat was cracked and dry. He dialed Jack after a short while.

"I'll take it," he cried. "Can you deliver it to my place?"

"Yes, but you will have to pay for delivery."

"Bring it, just bring it. I'll pay," he whimpered.

19.

Olivia

OLIVIA WALKED DOWN the aisle with her dad at her side. Her wedding gown flowed with her long hair as she walked.

Mzee Ajabu had gone out of his way to give her the wedding of her dreams. The garden at Muthaiga Country Club was decorated with white roses, and the chairs were lined with golden silk. Everybody looked cheerful, even Wairimu.

Olivia worked the aisle slowly, her hand clasped inside her dad's, making her feel like a little girl. Her feet stepped on red petals that her flower girl dropped ever so carefully. She looked at the congregation from the corners of her eyes. All the faces beamed with joy.

Larry stood with the pastor at the apex of the garden, waiting for his wife-to-be. He was dressed in a black tuxedo; his banking job ensured that he always looked dapper, but the tux made him look dashing. He smiled, and his face glowed.

His smile was her favorite of his features. Olivia would often stare at him when they were intertwined in bed or on the sofa just so he could look at her and ask, "What?" with that smile of his, and she would giggle and say, "Nothing."

Olivia took one step after another. Every step brought her closer to her husband-to-be. But she did not feel that way. She felt as if every step pulled her further away from him.

Olivia let go of her father's hand and increased her pace towards her husband-to-be. The flower girl couldn't keep up with her pace, and she got out of her way.

Walking quickly wasn't enough, and she rolled up her wedding gown and started running. As she ran, she started feeling as if someone was dragging a knife through her womb. She stopped and collapsed on the floor while holding her stomach. "Don't kill my son," she said, but nobody seemed to hear her. "Don't kill my son, I beg of you!" she shouted.

She lifted her head to look around the garden—everyone had left, including her family, and the white roses were bleeding. She tried to get up, but the pain in her stomach pinned her back down. She turned her gaze to her husband-to-be. He had been replaced by Dr. Onyango. Olivia woke up in her bed, screaming, her voice hoarse and tired.

20.

Mzee Ajabu

THEY STAYED IN the presidential suite of the Hilton Hotel at the Burj Khalifa, complete with their own chef and servants. Besides the golden chandelier and white drapes that adorned the suite, their room now had new décor: Ralph Lauren, Versace, Armani, and Dolce & Gabbana shopping bags sat on the mahogany table and leather seats.

Diana had washed, oiled, massaged, and clothed Mzee Ajabu, and they now stood on the balcony, marveling at a city that had grown out of a desert as James Brown's "It's a Man's, Man's, Man's World" filtered in softly through the balcony speakers. The sun had gone down and the different shades of lights from the city kissed them, making them look like movie stars.

Diana stretched her hand as if reaching towards the lights and took a photo. She had dressed the part too. She was in a white top that cut off just above her belly button and a flowy cotton miniskirt. Mzee Ajabu held her by the waist and dropped his hands to her plump buttocks.

"Take a photo of me with the backdrop of the city," Diana said excitedly while handing him her phone—the latest iPhone, unveiled less than a month ago. She posed this way and that, and Mzee Ajabu snapped.

"Sorry to disturb you. The chef is asking what you would like to have for dinner?" a waitress interrupted their photo shoot.

"What do you want to have, baby?" Mzee Ajabu asked Diana.

"I'll have smoked salmon and truffles," she said without a second thought.

"I'll have ugali, beef stew and *sukuma wiki*," Mzee Ajabu added.

The waitress bowed and dissolved behind the glass door.

It amused Mzee Ajabu how quickly Diana had evolved. When they met, she considered pizza and Kentucky Fried Chicken an extravagance, yet here she was, ordering smoked salmon and truffles as if they were her staple food.

He smiled and pulled her to him. The mention of food had given him other appetites.

"So, what's on the menu tomorrow, big man?" Diana asked when their eyes met.

"More shopping, more massages, more smoked salmon."

"Is that all?" Diana asked with a lewd smile.

"And more truffles," Mzee Ajabu said, turning her around. She arched her back out of habit, and he lifted the cotton miniskirt that was the only piece of fabric between him and what he wanted. She moaned softly to the sound of James Brown's voice, as the different shades of lights in the city of Dubai kissed them.

21.

Fred

Fred had burned through the money that was meant to pay for his music classes fast, and he now needed more. He waited until his mother was out of the house and walked into the master bedroom. The master bedroom was out of bounds to them, but he often found himself wandering there.

He walked past the king-size bed, into his mom's walk-in closet, and started rummaging through her clothes. She was an important man's wife, yet her closet was dull, Fred thought while going through the pockets of her coats and dresses.

When he did not find what he was looking for, he opened one drawer after another, removing and putting back his mother's undergarments. He looked through the shoe rack, which was full of flats and rubber shoes, opened some more drawers, and closed them in frustration.

He had seen his mother stepping out with the gold necklace and diamond-encrusted bracelet before, but now they were nowhere to be found. He went through the clothes and the drawers again before banging the door to his mom's closet behind him and walking towards his dad's closet.

His dad's closet looked like something out of a men's fashion magazine: custom-made suits hung inside it and boxes of shoes yet to be opened sat on the shelves.

In the corner of the closet was a safe. Fred leaned towards it and tried different combinations until it locked itself. He got up and rummaged through his dad's clothes, deciding he would revisit it later.

He did not search for long before finding what he was looking for—his dad's collection of watches: two Patek Philippes and a Rolex. *I should probably just take one,* he thought for a split second before taking all three and stuffing them into his pockets, complete with their cases.

A minute or so later, he was in his room. After hiding the watches, he started looking for his phone. He couldn't remember where he had put it. He beat his front and back pockets in small sporadic movements, murmuring, "Oh shit. Oh shit." He overturned his bedsheets, letting out a foul smell, before finding it under a bag of half-eaten crisps. He picked it up and dialed Jack.

22.

Olivia

OLIVIA STARED AT the meal of rice, chicken, and spinach her mom had brought into her room. She picked the spoon and took a small bite, then pushed it aside and fell back onto her pillow.

The four walls in her room started spinning, and everything went dark momentarily. She opened her eyes and she was with her husband, Larry. They were in the supermarket, shopping for baby items. They had just bought a beautiful pram and a gold-coated crib that made her beam with delight.

"I hope it's a boy," Larry said when they were at the clothes section of the supermarket, his demeanor dripping with urgency. There was a football game he was looking forward to later in the day.

"It will definitely be a boy," Olivia willed herself to please him.

"I'm sure you won't let me down," Larry replied with his face stuck on his phone.

Olivia looked away from him, realizing that a child's gender was not a matter in her control.

After shopping, they walked out of the supermarket with their fingers intertwined. Olivia was wearing a big smile; a supermarket attendant had just offered to push their trolley for them. Everything felt brand new to her. The people were nicer, even the air smelled better.

"We should name him after your dad," Olivia chirped.

Larry lifted his head momentarily. "My dad is a deadbeat. Let's name him after me. Larry Junior," he said and went back to his phone.

Olivia smiled and leaned on him as they entered the parking lot, where a blue Subaru Impreza was waiting for them. Larry had gotten it on loan, and he was still paying for it. He got out his keys and thumbed the alarm from a distance, and it made a sound, signaling the doors were now open.

They loaded the shopping into the boot and got inside the car. Larry turned on the ignition and started pulling out of the parking lot. They had not gone 10 meters when he slammed the breaks after hitting something. On the windshield of the Impreza lay Dr. Onyango, staring down at them with the look of death in his eyes. Olivia got up from her pillow, screaming.

23.

Mzee Ajabu

Mzee Ajabu's private jet touched down at Wilson Airport at 3:00 am. The first phone call he received was on his Kabambe, from his second lover, Helena. She was hysterical. Their daughter, Monica, was running amok at the club.

Monica could tell you clearly what it meant to live in the lap of luxury. She was only 19, and she drove a Porsche Cayenne and had a monthly allowance of 500,000 bob, which she burned on partying.

There wasn't a single club in Nairobi that did not know her by name. Her style was flamboyant and rowdy. She could spend upwards of 50,000 a night, and the night was usually incomplete if she had not caused chaos.

On this particular one, she was at the VIP lounge of a top club in the city with four of her friends. She had had her sights on this one boy, and she had been wooing him with drinks and trinkets the whole night. She was sure she would take him home, but after the third bottle of Johnnie Walker, the boy had caught the eye of a prettier girl, and he wanted nothing to do with her.

Monica was not ugly, but she wasn't beautiful either. She had a button nose, but her mouth was too wide. Her face was almost appealing but not quite. She could have complemented her looks with her figure, but she was the kind of woman who gained weight rapidly if she did not watch what she was eating, and Monica had no time for watching. If she wanted it, she got it.

"You dumb bitch. Do you know who I am?" Monica had barked at the girl, who was now looking at her, confused. She found herself breaking a bottle of Johnnie Walker on the table and cutting her with it. "That should teach you not to steal people's men," she had roared as blood gushed out of the girl's head where her ear was meant to be.

The bouncers of the club swooped in and carried Monica away. "Fuck you! My father will hear about this!" she barked some more while kicking her legs.

Mzee Ajabu had fallen in love with her mother the moment he had laid eyes on her. He had been so taken by her beauty that he had opened a beauty spa in the city for her, to supplement her TV-show-host income, even though all it seemed to do nowadays was empty his pockets.

Helena had gotten pregnant with Monica just after Fred was born, and they had decided that she was a love child. Part of being a love child meant she got everything she wanted.

Mzee Ajabu stared at his phone after he was done talking to Helena. He thought of calling Monica and chastising her but thought against it. He knew his words would fall on deaf ears; that was if she picked his call and stayed quiet for long enough without calling him a deadbeat dad.

He scrolled through his contact list, and in less than a minute, he was talking to the owner of the club. Within seconds, the bleeding girl was being escorted out of the club by bouncers while crying, and Monica was in her Porsche Cayenne being driven home. Back in the club, the CCTV footage was being destroyed. The incident was non-existent—it had never happened.

24.

Love Child

Monica woke up at noon with a terrible hangover, but even the hangover did not feel as bad as the void she felt within herself. She dragged herself out of bed and looked in the mirror. She had big eyebags underneath her eyes. "Not today, Monica. Not today," she murmured to herself while splashing water on her face to try and flatten them.

She toweled off, held her braids in a ponytail, and went to the sitting room. "Mom, Mom, Mom," she called. She often forgot that her mom was always at work or at an event or a cocktail party. She went to the kitchen, downed two Mara Moja pills with a glass of water, and went looking for breakfast in the fridge.

There was a note on the fridge: 'Hey sunshine, won't be back till late at night. There's some leftover pizza in the microwave. Love, Mom.' The note was signed off with love hearts. Monica poured herself a glass of mango juice, warmed the pizza, and went to eat it in their gazebo.

She appreciated how her relationship with her mother felt like an intimate friendship or as if they were roommates, but sometimes she wondered if she would have this void within her if she lived a normal life with normal parents like most children.

She took a swig from her glass and stared at their muscled shamba-boy working on their lawn. Their eyes met, and he smiled. She averted her eyes. It had happened one drunken afternoon, and she had regretted it the next morning. She raised her gaze and stared at him again—her mother knew how to select them, she thought while getting up and going to her bedroom.

Her hangover had ebbed, but the void seemed to have grown in size. "Not today, Monica. Not today," she murmured to herself again. Her mother had enrolled her for a stage play at the Kenya National Theatre while she waited to go to college. She picked up the script from her dresser and read it. It was about a girl who had forgotten who she was and was now finding redemption in her passion for dancing.

She stared at the script, and her mind went still. She stared at it without reading it. What if her dad was in her life? Would she still feel this empty? she wondered. She placed the script back on the dresser and got up from her bed to practice the dancing steps.

"One, two, three, four. Then spin. Five, six, seven. Then bend. Eight, nine, and ten. Stand and spin." She sat on her bed, breathing hard, realizing she was too unfit to be the star of the play.

The realization made the void grow even bigger. She found herself going to her bag and coming out with a syringe, a small bag of white powder, cotton wool, and a lighter.

She put a bit of the powder on a spoon and added a few drops of water before heating it with the lighter. She pinched a small piece of cotton wool and soaked it in the liquid before filling a quarter of the syringe. She tightened her hairband around her upper arm and emptied the contents into her vein. "Not today, Monica, not today," she murmured as the world went dark around her.

25.

Diana

DIANA SAT ON her queen bed in her Lavington apartment and opened her photo gallery. It was littered with images from her Dubai trip. She picked one where she was holding designer shopping bags and posted it on her Instagram profile. *Work hard, play harder,* she captioned it and continued scrolling through her gallery.

She stopped at a photo of her sitting in Mzee Ajabu's private jet, holding a glass of sparkling wine, in a dress that exposed her yellow thighs. *Boss babe vibes,* she captioned the photo and tapped the post button.

She tapped on her profile and edited her bio from, *Welcome to my photo album* to *Entrepreneur and Boss Lady,* and deleted all the shabby photos from her timeline. She then updated her stories with the photo of her hand reaching towards the lights. *Chasing heights and lights in Dubai. Boss Babe Vibes.* She hit post, picked her phone, and went to the kitchen.

Her house-help had made muffins, jacket potatoes, tea, and sausages. She fixed herself a plate and went to the sitting room. She sat on the sofa, picked up the remote, switched to *E!*, and started watching *Keeping up with the Kardashians* while having breakfast.

It was noon when she got up from the sofa. She had forgotten to go for her Public Relations classes again. She stared at her class notes and felt the fingers of a migraine start to climb up the back of her spine. She put her coursework aside and dialed Mzee Ajabu.

"Have you missed me?" she asked while twirling her braids.

"Let me call you in a minute," the voice on the other end said.

"Imagine I don't think Public Relations is for me," Diana said after Mzee Ajabu called back.

"What do you want to do?"

"I am not sure yet, but I don't think it's Public Relations."

"Don't stress yourself. When you figure it out, tell me and I will sort it out."

"You're so sweet."

"Anything for you. Is something else stressing you?"

"Nothing for now, but I could do with some pocket money and cuddles."

"I will send you something and visit you soon. Be a good girl till then."

"Be a good boy too," she giggled and thumbed the red receiver button.

Ten minutes did not pass before her phone trilled with an M-pesa message. Diana looked at the message and beamed. Mzee Ajabu had just sent her 100,000 bob. She called her house-help and told her not to bother with lunch because she was stepping out. She sat on her sofa and watched three more episodes of *Keeping up with the Kardashians* before getting up and going to have a shower.

She wore a Dolce & Gabbana cocktail dress, picked up her BMW X1 keys, and headed to the Villa Rosa Kempinski hotel. The sun was going down when she sat down with her meal of crispy fish with sweet and sour sauce and a glass of gin and tonic. *You are what you eat,* she captioned a photo of her plate and updated her Instagram stories.

26.

Wairimu

WAIRIMU DID NOT imagine her first day of work would go like this. She was the boss's daughter; she would most certainly get a managerial position, maybe even a small office to start off. She had decided she needed to look the part.

She had gone shopping with the 10,000 bob her mother had given her after she told her she didn't have office wear. Mrs. Ajabu had hesitated before sending her the money. "Don't buy clothes that show your breasts. It's an office, not a demonstration," she had told her.

Wairimu had gone to Toi Market and spent 3,000 bob on a few dresses whose hems went below her knees, cheap earrings, and three pairs of high heels—they would make her tower and intimidate some men in the office, she had thought and grinned. She saved the rest of the money for fare and lunch for the month.

She got home and tried on the clothes. She looked decent, not elegant like she had wanted. That would all change after she got her salary. "100,000; 200,000; 300,000?" She smiled. She could even move out and bring her sister with her.

Wairimu got into a matatu in the morning, and within the hour, she was walking through the revolving doors of the Mirage Tower, headed to Ajabu Digital.

The Chief Operating Officer, Mr. Kitana, welcomed her warmly to his office. The citrus in his perfume burned her nostrils. She glanced at him. He was of average height, lean, with a face that exuded intelligence.

His office was second to Mzee Ajabu's, but it was also grand, with a big mahogany desk, a meeting area, and a breathtaking view of Nairobi. Wairimu looked at it with envy and wondered why she had refused to start her job sooner.

After introductions, they sat in the meeting area for debriefing.

"You will be reporting to my assistant. Your work will start at eight in the morning," Kitana's tone had changed from warm to business-like. "You will pick newspapers from the reception desk and ferry them to me, to the CEO, CFO, CHRO...Uhmm, I can't name them all—the receptionist will guide you."

"After that, you will sit at your desk and sort out the inventory for the day. What is needed in every department in matters stationery: pens, notebooks, markers, etc. My assistant will guide you," he said and glanced at her, the color had drained from her face. "That will be your job from around 10:00 am till you clock out at 5:00 pm. Any questions?"

"Does my dad know about this?" Wairimu coughed in a high-pitched tone.

"They are his orders, miss," Kitana replied sternly.

"And my salary?"

"We will start you off with a gross income of 20,000 bob; that will be around 18,000 after taxes." He paused, waiting for her to respond, but her mouth had formed an 'O' instead. "If there is nothing else, the receptionist and my assistant will take it from here."

Wairimu got up, smoothed her dress, took her handbag, got out of the office, and headed towards the reception desk. It was a big, plush desk, and an equally plush woman who was very pregnant sat behind it. Beside the desk was a pile of newspapers that could serve as a nightstand.

Wairimu glanced at the exit for what felt like a minute before picking up a newspaper.

"Where do these go?" she asked the woman.

"Oh, you're the new intern. I'm Tatiana, *karibu sana*," she said while extending her hand for a handshake.

"I'm Wairimu, nice to meet you," Wairimu said, the color draining from her face further as they shook hands.

"Come, let me show you around," the receptionist said while smiling, happy that the task of ferrying newspapers was no longer hers.

27.

Olivia

OLIVIA SAT ON the couch, propped up by pillows. Her skin was pale, and her clothes sagged on her body. She had just taken two bites of the *chapati* and beef stew that sat in front of her before pushing it away.

She stared at the huge chandelier and the fan making its rounds on the ceiling. The air from the fan swayed the crystals on the chandelier, making them clink. Olivia watched the fan rotate again and again and listened to the clinking sounds until her mind went numb, and then everything went quiet.

Clink, clink, clink. Her mother was hitting a wine glass with a spoon. "I wish Larry Junior health and wealth," she said before taking a seat.

"I wish him looks and smarts," a family friend was saying.

"May he be as good-hearted as his mother," another one had stood up to say.

Olivia looked around. They were in the backyard of their

house. People were drinking, eating, and making merry, and they all seemed to be women.

Clink, clink, clink. Wairimu was hitting her glass with a spoon. "It's time for Mama Larry Junior to open her presents. Let's give Olivia a round of applause as she comes forward."

Olivia was just now noticing the pink ribbon running from her shoulder to her waist written 'Mother-To-Be' in white and realizing that it was her baby shower. She got up slowly and stared at the overwhelming number of boxes that were waiting for her to unwrap. "Don't be shy; open them. They are yours," Wairimu said, and the whole backyard was filled with laughter.

Olivia unwrapped the first gift. It was a set of burp cloths from a family friend. The family friend got up. "Larry Junior might look cute when he arrives but believe me, what comes out of his mouth won't be." The whole backyard was uproarious as the family friend took her seat.

The second gift was a baby monitor from Wairimu. "This will help you make sure Larry Junior is okay without being near him all the time; for those days when you want time to yourself or quality time with Baba Larry Junior," she said and winked, and the whole backyard giggled.

The third gift astonished her. It was a short, sharp knife from her mother. She picked it up and inspected it as her mother got up to speak. She lifted her head to hear what she would say and realized that the backyard was now empty, except for her mother, who was growing in height as she stood.

She rubbed her eyes and opened them again, and her mother had been replaced by Dr. Onyango. He grabbed the knife from Olivia's hands and started stabbing her belly with it. One time, two times, three times, countless times. "Stop! Stop! Stop killing my son!" Olivia woke up screaming as the fan made its rounds on the ceiling and the chandelier crystals clinked.

28.

Boys Will Be Boys

BOYS WILL BE BOYS. It is the way they were made. It showed their virility and mettle, and it was in that way that Mrs. Ajabu didn't say anything when Fred started smoking and drinking alcohol when he was still in primary school.

She felt that he was now on the path to becoming a real man. She would sometimes leave her husband's bottle of Jack Daniel's carelessly in the house just so he could stumble upon it and become more of a man.

He switched from cigarettes and alcohol to miraa after a while. It was a disgusting habit that annoyed Mrs. Ajabu. It gave his mouth a nasty green color, and besides that, he started keeping questionable company. Boys will be boys, Mrs. Ajabu reminded herself.

Fred picked up bhang right after he joined campus. He had been a good performer even with the distractions, but after a few puffs of weed, he dropped out of college to pursue a career in music, and that was how he found himself nose-deep in powder.

It's just another phase, Mrs. Ajabu had convinced herself after she went to her husband's closet and found the watches missing. "Boys will be boys," she had reminded herself, and she replaced them with knock-offs.

***

She was seated on the sofa watching Telemundo and drinking from her large glass of wine when she decided that maybe their closets needed new locks. She picked her wine and went to their master bedroom to inspect the doors. It was then that she realized her husband's safe had been broken into.

She eavesdropped on her husband's conversations with his Chief Financial Officer every now and again, and she had heard him say more than once that he kept over a million shillings in his home safe.

Mrs. Ajabu dropped her wine glass and ran towards Fred's bedroom. She had not been in his room since he was a teenager. Fred liked it that way. She knocked again and again until she couldn't stand her anxiety anymore, and she got the spare key to his room and opened the door.

Immediately she pushed open the door, a stench hit her like a mallet, followed by shock. There was white powder on the table, and her son lay like a lifeless thing on his bed. She approached him and shook him gently. "Fred. Fred. My son," she pleaded. Fred coughed, and white froth bubbled up his mouth, and he started choking.

Mrs. Ajabu supported him with a pillow and ran to her phone to dial their family doctor. In less than half an hour, she was tearing up in an ambulance headed for Nairobi Hospital, staring at her son as Dr. Onyango zapped him with defibrillators, trying to resuscitate him. Mrs. Ajabu felt physical pain every

73

time the defibrillator came into contact with her son's body and zapped his chest.

"Will he make it?" she asked. "Please do everything you can to bring him back," she begged as tears ran down her face. Another shock wave hit her son, and she became light-headed. It was as she was falling into unconsciousness that she realized that when boys wanted to be boys, you shouldn't always allow them.

29.

Monica

MONICA WOKE UP in the evening the next day with a migraine. She was in the mood for fun today. She went to the kitchen, downed two Mara Moja pills with a glass of water, and opened the fridge for a glass of mango juice. There was another note on the door with love hearts drawn on the side. 'Hi sunshine, did not want to wake you. Enjoy your day. Love, Mom.'

She went to the gazebo with her glass of mango juice. She sat down, and the void opened up in her again. "Not today, Monica. Not today," she murmured while lifting her gaze to their garden. Their shamba-boy was still out there, working on their hedges. Their eyes met, and Monica got up and entered their house.

She sat on the sofa and texted her four friends, 'Let's party tonight…' She stared at the phone. 'My treat,' she added finally before hitting send.

She wore a shower cap and soaked in the bathtub while shaving her legs before rinsing off in the shower. She toweled off and put on a provocative purple miniskirt, red bottoms, and Lancôme perfume.

When she was done with her makeup, she removed her hairband, and her braids fell down her back. *Tonight won't be another lonely night,* she thought while picking her handbag and car keys. She stopped momentarily, as if she had forgotten something, and put the script in her bag. She got into her Porsche Cayenne and drove off, leaving their shamba-boy working on their hedges.

***

"We missed you so much."

"You're glowing."

"I love your shoes."

"That dress is gorg."

Monica's friends sang while getting up from their regular seats and following her to the VIP section of the club. There were three bottles of Johnnie Walker sitting in a bucket of ice and strawberry and vanilla-flavored shisha bongs on the table.

"I think the handsome guy at the counter is checking you out," one of her friends said after taking a long pull from the strawberry-flavored shisha bong and spitting pink smoke from her nostrils.

"He totally is," another friend giggled, spitting white smoke from her nostrils.

The guy in question was tall and muscled, with dreadlocks and a brown goatee. He was in a simple shirt, denim trousers, and sneakers. He had been checking out Monica for a while now. He particularly loved her flamboyant lifestyle. He leaned on the counter, toyed with his finger of Johnnie Walker, and stole another glance.

"What are you going to do?" the third one asked while sipping her drink.

"Oh my God, oh my God." The fourth one moved her hands in a flurry.

"Compliments from the gentleman with dreadlocks at the counter," a waitress was saying while presenting Monica with a bottle of Johnnie Walker.

The dress was doing wonders. *Tonight won't be another lonely night,* she thought again while getting up and walking towards him.

"What is a girl like you doing in a place like this?" he asked.

She giggled. She was now realizing that he was an older man. She was always being approached by younger boys. This was a welcome change. She giggled again.

"Do you have any plans after this?"

"No, not really," she said while playing with her braids.

"I am just about to get out of here. Do you want to join me?"

"Okay, let me tell my friends goodbye."

They got out of the club. "I came with an Uber; you don't mind if I drive your Porsche, do you?"

Monica had thought he had his own car, and she had planned to leave her car at the club and come for it the next morning. "That works perfectly," she said while handing him the keys. She got into the passenger's seat as he got into the driver's seat, and they drove off.

30.

Wairimu

WAIRIMU STOOD NEXT to Tatiana in the lift while balancing newspapers on her hands, trying to make sure none of them fell and at the same time trying not to fall flat on her face in her high heels. Flats would have been a better investment, she was realizing with chagrin as the lift dinged open on the first floor where the human resources offices were located.

The Chief Human Resource Officer was a lean woman who wore round horn-rimmed glasses. She did not so much as look at Wairimu; she just nodded after Wairimu placed her newspapers on her desk and got back to her MacBook.

She walked with Tatiana to the acquisition and research offices. Both managers were not in. Wairimu folded their newspapers in half and placed them on their desks, and they headed back to the lifts.

"People say the HR boss was left by her husband for his secretary; that's why she is so bitter," Tatiana whispered in Wairimu's ear while rubbing her tremendous belly after the lifts closed.

Wairimu stared at her, astonished.

"After that, she fired her own secretary."

Wairimu's mouth was now open.

"Just place the newspapers on her desk and leave quickly if you don't want to get on her wrong side," Tatiana added as the lift dinged open on the fifth floor, where the creative offices were located.

There were nine creative directors—including the Chief Creative Officer—eight account directors, and four social media managers. Wairimu was relieved that none of them had clocked in. She placed the newspapers on their desks hurriedly, and they went back to the lifts and headed for the seventh floor, where the Information Technology offices were.

"How come the creative department heads haven't clocked in?" she asked Tatiana and immediately regretted doing so.

"They are bosses, and we are foot soldiers," she said flatly as the lift dinged open once more.

The seventh floor housed the Chief Technology Officer, IT Manager, Systems Architect, and Software Engineer. They were all busy in their offices. They said hello when she placed their newspapers on their desks and went back to clicking their keyboards. The only one who was warm was the software engineer. A short, balding guy with an intelligent face. He introduced himself and thanked her for the newspapers, and for some reason, her job felt important.

"Stay away from Chris. He is a known womanizer," Tatiana was whispering into Wairimu's ear after the lifts had closed.

"Wairimu gave her the same astonished face.

"I can't begin to tell you the number of women in this organization who have flushed his kids," she added while rubbing her belly again, and Wairimu's jaw dropped.

"Stay away from him. He is a well-known hit-and-run," she whispered as the lift dinged on the ninth floor. It was the topmost floor, where her father and all the heavy hitters of the organization were located, and where she would be sitting.

The Chief Operation Officer, Chief Information Officer, Chief Financial Officer, Head of Credit Control, and Head of Debtors were all in meetings, Tatiana had told her. Her father, who had not been seen in the office lately, was the only one missing. The receptionist did not have any gossip about her dad. *I suppose she knows which side of her bread is buttered and not to bite the hand that feeds her,* Wairimu thought.

She folded the newspapers in half, placed them on her father's desk, and stared at his empty chair. She had not seen him in a while, she realized, and wondered if someone else had beaten her to her revenge mission. She closed his office door behind her and went to place the newspapers on the desks of the other offices, and she breathed a sigh of relief after she was done.

The clock read 9:00 am. She started walking to the water dispenser. All that walking and gossip had made her hot and she needed a glass of water to cool down, but before she could make it to the dispenser, she heard a voice behind her.

"You're Wairimu, right?" the Assistant COO asked. "Your computer has been set up," she continued before she could respond. "I need you to key in the documents at your desk into the system." She looked at her workstation. The desktop was dwarfed by a pile of papers. She wanted to run back home, but instead, she turned and walked slowly towards her desk.

31.

Helena

Mzee Ajabu lay exhausted in the queen bed in the villa of his second lover in the suburbs of Karen. To his left was a big glass door leading to the balcony, where Helena was smoking a cigarette. Mzee Ajabu groaned and thought of getting out of bed and telling her to put it out. He groaned again and decided to let her enjoy herself.

Helena was in a lacy thong and a silk gown that exposed her breasts. She stubbed out the cigarette on the balcony railing, dropped it into the wastebasket, and popped a mint into her mouth.

She leaned against the rails and felt the breeze massage her body while she enjoyed the view of her backyard. Below the balcony, her shamba-boy was trimming the hedges. They made eye contact for what felt like a minute before Helena closed her gown and walked back to Mzee Ajabu with a smile on her face.

"Did you miss me?" she asked and planted a kiss on his

mouth.

Mzee Ajabu pulled her to him and kissed her hard; she pulled away after some time.

"Thank you for sorting out Monica," she chirped.

"She's a handful, isn't she?"

"She is, but she's my daughter and I love her."

"She's my daughter too," Mzee Ajabu said defensively, even though there were days when he had his doubts. Her mouth and her face were not in his family tree—perhaps they belonged to a relative on Helena's side, he reasoned.

"Where is she?" he asked after a moment's silence.

"I have no idea." Helena paused as if searching her mind for her whereabouts. "You know how teenagers can be," she added, getting into her nightstand drawer and removing a packet of Embassy Lights and a lighter. "Speaking of your daughter, her allowance has run out; mine too. The rent is also due, and Helena Beauty Spa needs supplies."

"I thought you told me your business would be profitable this year?" Mzee Ajabu asked, his tone almost the one he used to address his subordinates.

Helena placed the packet of cigarettes and the lighter on the nightstand and planted another kiss on Mzee Ajabu's mouth. Then she sat back and started massaging his chest.

"You know how business is. Sometimes it's up, other times it's down," she said in a husky, erotic whisper.

"How much do you need?"

"Three million shillings only. A million for our upkeep and two million for the house and the business."

"Okay, I will wire you the money when I get to the office. But you need to come up with a plan for your business."

"Thanks for understanding," Helena said and planted another kiss on his lips. She picked her packet of Embassy Lights, lit a cigarette, and took a long pull. *Should she call her shamba-boy after Mzee Ajabu had left? Her house plants needed watering,* she thought and blew a cloud of smoke into the air.

Mzee Ajabu groaned and got out of bed.

"You're leaving already?" she asked.

"I haven't seen my family in over a week, and I need to put some things in order at the office," Mzee Ajabu said while putting on his trousers.

"Come back to bed?" Helena pleaded after blowing another cloud of smoke into the air.

"If I stay any longer, things will go wrong," Mzee Ajabu said, putting on his shirt and shoes.

"I will miss you," Helena said, stubbing out her cigarette on the ashtray and getting out of bed. She picked up his coat and followed him to the door.

"Don't forget about me," she said while helping him put it on.

"How can I forget such beauty?" Mzee Ajabu said and kissed her hard before she pulled away.

"I will be looking forward to your message," she said finally and watched him walking to his Range Rover and driving off. Helena stood at the door momentarily before closing it and walking towards her balcony.

32.

One Night Stand

Monica ran her fingers through her club flame's brown goatee. "I like your style," she groaned while lying on his hairy chest. They were at a lodging in downtown Nairobi. "What is this place?" Monica asked after her eyes adjusted to the light.

"Are you hungry?" he changed the topic.

"I'm starving."

"I can get us breakfast, but I forgot my wallet at the club."

They stayed quiet for a while.

"I'll get you back," he said finally.

"Hand me my bag on the table."

He handed her the bag and watched her removing a crisp 1,000-shilling note from a stack of many.

"How much money do you usually carry in your bag?" he asked, surprised, as Monica handed him the money.

"Not much; about 50 to 100,000 bob when I'm going out, sometimes more."

He looked at her in shock, picked the money, and got out of the room. Immediately he left, Monica felt the immense void open up inside her. "Not today, Monica, not today," she told herself. She got into her bag, removed her script, and tried to practice the dancing steps.

"One, two, three, four. Then spin. Five, six, seven. Then bend. Eight, nine, and ten. Stand and spin." She sat back on the bed, breathing hard. She lay down and wondered if she would be in a dingy lodging with a man she barely knew if she had a normal family. She felt the void open further and got up and went to her bag again.

The door flew open before she could get what she wanted. Her flame walked in, holding a tray with two cups of tea, sausages, and *mandazi*. She put the script back in her bag and sat beside him.

She broke a sausage in two and threw one half into her mouth before picking her cup of tea.

They started kissing halfway through breakfast, and then she was holding the headboard of the bed and moaning softly as he took her from behind.

"How good is your car alarm system?" he asked while removing the condom and throwing it in the wastebasket.

"I'm not sure; my mom sorted it out."

"I deal with top-of-the-line car alarm systems. I can hook you up."

Monica got into her handbag again, came out with a hairband, and held her braids in a ponytail.

"In case of anything, I will give you a ring."

"Oh, okay," he said, and Monica felt the emptiness hit her again.

"Hold me," she asked him, and he did.

"Squeeze me close to you." He put his big arms around her.

"Don't let me go," she added.

They stayed that way for a while before Monica spoke again.

"I have something that could make us feel even closer; want to try?"

The man nodded.

She got into her bag again and came out with a lighter, a syringe, a bottle of water, cotton wool, and a bag of powder. She heated the contents on one of the teaspoons, soaked cotton wool in the liquid, filled a quarter of the syringe, and moved towards him with the pointed end."

"It's okay; I will inject myself after you do."

She looked at him, removed her hairband, and tightened it around her upper arm. She stuck the needle in her vein and emptied its contents into her body. "Not today, Monica. Not today," he heard her murmur as her head hit the pillow.

After she blacked out, the man poured all the powder remaining in the bag onto the spoon, heated it up, and filled the syringe. He stuck the needle in Monica's neck and emptied its contents into her body. He then took her car keys and the money in her bag and left the lodging.

33.

Tennis

DIANA WAS AT the tennis court for her tennis training. This was her second time at the court. Mzee Ajabu had suggested it after she told him Public Relations wasn't for her.

"Everything is arranged. You can do the training twice a week," he had told her.

Diana had hesitated, then she had remembered watching the Kardashians playing the game, and she had agreed.

"Hold the racket with your right hand," the trainer was saying. "Stand behind the service line." He was going behind her and positioning her correctly. "Finish the stroke from the contact of the ball to the back of your left shoulder," he said finally.

Diana stood behind the service line and took a swing at the tennis ball like she had been instructed. The ball flew out of the court into the trees. The trainer was back behind her, positioning her again.

"Don't hit it too hard. Your job is to get the ball inside the court," he said.

She glanced at him; he was middle-aged, balding, with a beer gut. She averted her eyes from him and took a softer swing as he had instructed.

They took a 15-minute break, and Diana got her phone and asked him to take a photo of her. She was in a white tank top, purple tennis miniskirt, white socks, and white sneakers. They all had the Nike swoosh logo on them. *Wishing you love and light today #OOTD,* she captioned the photo and posted it on her Instagram profile.

It was noon when she finished her training session. She went to the changing room, had a shower, toweled, and lotioned. She wore tight-fitting, blue denim trousers, a mustard Ralph Lauren waterfall cardigan, and brown sandals. She looked into the mirror and held her hair into a ponytail. She took a mirror selfie. *I woke up like this,* she captioned the photo and shared it on her Instagram stories.

She packed her tennis gear into her backpack, picked up her car keys, and headed for lunch. She was seated at Artcaffé in less than half an hour, having chicken shawarma with orange juice. She took a photo of the food: *50 Shades of Foodie,* she captioned it and shared it on her stories.

She finished her day by going to Helena Beauty Spa. She took a selfie with the establishment in the background. *Time to be pampered. #BossBabeVibes,* she captioned the photo and shared it on her Instagram stories.

34.

Helena Beauty Spa

AFTER HER MASSAGE, hair touch-up, and manicure, Diana walked in her white bathrobe to the pedicure room of Helena Beauty Spa to find two other women being attended to. One was very pregnant and the other one looked familiar, she noticed.

"Will you have coffee or wine?" a lady asked her after she sat down.

"Do you have green tea?" she asked.

"Yes," the lady replied.

"I will have that," Diana said as the pedicurist placed her feet on her lap and started clipping her nails.

She looked at the familiar lady to her right, through the corner of her eye, and remembered where she had seen her—on TV, hosting a show.

"You're Helena?" she thought without knowing she was saying the words out loud.

"Guilty," she said nonchalantly.

"Don't be fooled by her humbleness; she's also the owner of this establishment," her pregnant friend said loudly. "You better know people in this town, especially if you want free pedicures, child," she added.

"What's your name?" Helena asked with half a smile.

"I'm Diana. It's nice to meet you, Helana. I watch your show," she replied meekly as the pedicurist filed her toenails.

"You don't have to be so nice, Diana. This is a safe space—let loose. Tell us about your boyfriend or boyfriends," Helena's pregnant friend said and giggled.

Diana blushed as her green tea arrived, and she took a tiny sip.

"Diana, meet my friend, Tatiana. The one thing she loves more than free pedicures *ni mushene*. You don't have to tell us about your boyfriend," Helena added and chuckled.

"Unless you want to," Tatiana said and laughed again.

"I'm…I'm in campus," Diana stammered as the pedicurist applied cuticle gel on her toenails and dipped her feet in a footbath of warm water.

"Campus girls are the ones stealing our men nowadays," Tatiana said.

"Come on, Tatiana, be nice. Tell her about the church you were telling me about," Helena said.

"Oh, Nairobi Revival Church. You can check it out," Tatiana got into her handbag and handed them pamphlets.

"Are they paying you to recruit people?" Helena asked, and they all laughed.

"Something like that." She winked, and they all laughed again.

"Can I take a selfie with y'all?" Diana asked, a bit bolder now, while reaching into her bathrobe pocket and coming out with her phone.

"Let me touch up my lipstick," Tatiana said.

"I'm always camera-ready," Helena boasted.

Hanging out with Helena Beauty Spa Boss Lady. Great minds think alike. #CoolAunties. Diana captioned the photo and posted it on her Instagram profile.

"You remind me a lot of my daughter, Monica. She's about your age. She's getting ready to join campus too," Helena said proudly.

"Oh, really? Tell her I said hello," Diana said after taking a sip from her green tea as the pedicurist applied massage oil on her legs and started kneading her calves.

Helena's phone started ringing. She picked it and replied with mmh's and uh's. After the call, Diana noticed the color had drained from her face, and her demeanor had sagged.

"What's wrong, hon?" Tatiana asked.

"It's Monica," Helena said, wearing her slippers and rushing out of the room.

Tatiana asked her pedicurist to dry her feet and followed her.

Diana finished her tea as her pedicurist applied pink nail polish on her toenails. She removed her phone and took another selfie. *Physically in Nairobi, mentally in Dubai,* she captioned it and shared it on her Instagram stories.

35.

Mrs. Ajabu

Mrs. Ajabu woke up from unconsciousness to find her son on the hospital bed with a gas mask strapped on his face, tubes running throughout his upper body like a network of wires, and his chest moving up and down to the beeping sound of a cardiac monitor.

"Your son is lucky. Most patients don't survive a drug overdose of this proportion," Dr. Onyango was telling her, and she was gawking at him as if in a trance.

Fred opened his eyes. His mom was standing with her back to him. He went to talk, but his throat was dry. He could hear chattering, but he couldn't make out the words. He felt tired, as if he had run a marathon. He closed his eyes and went back to sleep.

"He is now stable. We pumped the drugs out of his system and put him on antibiotics. He is going to need plenty of water and a lot of rest. I would advocate for a rehabilitation facility after he has recuperated."

"Doctor, I don't want any of this getting to his father," Mrs. Ajabu was now saying after coming back to her senses.

"I don't need to tell you that I know what goes on in your private clinic," she added.

"My lips are sealed," Dr. Onyango said while making a zip-up gesture on his mouth with his thumb and forefinger. "I won't even charge you for this, but your son needs rehabilitation, and that will come with a cost. It might be in your best interest to tell his father."

"Give me contacts to a good rehab center, and let me worry about the money," Mrs. Ajabu said curtly. She knew her husband had him on a good retainer, and the services he had performed today were a small price to pay.

Dr. Onyango got into his file and handed her a card. "Give them a call; they are based in Nanyuki. They are very good."

Mrs. Ajabu took the card and stared at the name Meadows Rehabilitation Facility that was written on it.

"After you are decided, give me a call, and I will arrange for him to be airlifted there after he recuperates."

"Thank you," she said for the first time throughout her interaction with him.

"No problem. If there is nothing else, I will leave you to your son. I'm sure you want to spend time with him." She nodded, and Dr. Onyango walked to the door and closed it behind him.

Mrs. Ajabu turned and looked at her son. The color was starting to return to his face. She sat next to him and wondered how she would make up for the money that was missing from the safe and pay for the rehabilitation facility. And then it came to her.

She would sell the golden necklace and diamond-encrusted

bracelet that Mzee Ajabu had gifted her on their 20th anniversary. They didn't hold any sentimental value to her, she was realizing.

They would fetch anywhere from 1.5 to 2 million Kenya shillings. She would get the safe fixed and make sure she got the codes to it and put a million back. That would be enough to throw off her husband's scent, and she could put the rest towards her son's recuperation.

If the safe contained more money, she would act clueless, she decided; after all, her husband did not involve her in his business. A smile almost touched her face as she got back to staring at her son's chest moving up and down to the beeping sound of the cardiac monitor.

36.

Olivia

OLIVIA GOT UP at noon. She dragged herself to the kitchen and looked at the leftover rice, beef, and steamed cabbage that had been cooked the previous night. She did not bother heating it up. She fixed herself a plate and went with it to the sitting room.

The fan had been switched off. The golden chandelier hung sentry on the ceiling, as if watching her. She took a spoonful of the food, then another, but before she could lift the third spoonful to her mouth, the room started spinning, and then it went dark.

She was on a stretcher, being wheeled to the delivery room.

"Is it a boy?" she inquired.

"Breathe," the nurse that was pushing her stretcher said.

"Please tell me, is it a boy? Is it a boy?" she was shouting now.

"We will know in a few minutes; just breathe," the nurse said.

The delivery room doors flew open, and she was wheeled to the center of the room where the doctor was waiting.

"Push. Push. Push." She was sweating profusely and trying her best to do what she was being told. "You're not pushing. Push," the doctor's voice boomed. She gathered all her energy and screamed loudly while she pushed with all her strength.

"Good job," the doctor said.

"Is it a boy?" she inquired again.

The room was silent besides the crying of her baby. It was as if the doctor and the nurse could not hear her. She felt as if she was drowning in a pool and trying to speak to the people outside it.

"Please tell me, is it a boy? Is it a boy?" She was shouting again.

The nurse finished cleaning the baby and walked towards her. "You have given birth to a bouncing baby girl," she said. Olivia heard the words as if in slow motion. Her husband, Larry, wouldn't be happy, she knew.

She reached for her baby, but before she could, the nurse took her from her. "I need to clean her and clothe her." She turned towards Olivia, and she saw her place a stethoscope on her tiny chest.

Olivia blinked, and the nurse had turned into Dr. Onyango. Instead of a stethoscope, he was holding a knife, and he was now stabbing her daughter: one time, two times, three times, countless times. She let out a horrid scream and woke up in their living room—her plate and its contents of rice, beef, and steamed cabbage on the floor.

37.

Mrs. Ajabu

Mrs. Ajabu served her husband a meal of *ugali*, *sukuma wiki*, and beef stew for supper after he arrived. She brought him a bowl of warm water and a towel. After he was done washing his hands and toweling off, she took the bowl and towel back to the kitchen, came back to the sitting room, and sat beside him.

Mzee Ajabu rolled his sleeves, pinched a chunk of *ugali*, scooped some meat together with some *sukuma wiki*, and took a bite. "How have things been going around here," he asked after swallowing the bite."

"Nothing much," Mrs. Ajabu paused. "Wairimu started going to work," she added.

"That will be good for her. She will stop giving us a headache."

"I gave her some money to buy decent clothes for the office."

Mzee Ajabu pinched another chunk of *ugali* and scooped

some meat and *sukuma wiki*. "How much did you give her?"

"30,000 shillings."

"I will send some money into your account when I get to work tomorrow."

Mrs. Ajabu moved on her seat to get comfortable and glanced at her husband's plate. He had cleared the *sukuma wiki*. "Do you want some more *sukuma*?" she asked.

"Yes. Add some more beef stew too," he said while handing her his plate.

Mrs. Ajabu disappeared into the kitchen and came back with a full plate.

"The *sukuma wiki* is very good," Mzee Ajabu remarked after taking another bite.

"I have a lady who brings them fresh from the farm."

He pinched another chunk of *ugali*. "How are Olivia and Fred?" he asked.

"Olivia is asleep. She has been helping me around the house—she prepared the *sukuma*."

"That's my girl," he said after swallowing the bite. "What about Fred?"

"He's in Nanyuki for an entrepreneurship seminar with his finance class.

Mzee Ajabu nodded his head while wiping his plate clean with a chunk of *ugali*. "That will be good for him."

Mrs. Ajabu took the empty plate and disappeared to the kitchen again. She came back with a fresh bowl of warm water and a fresh towel.

"Speaking of Fred, his graduation is coming up," she said. "We will need to throw a small party for him," she added.

"How much will it cost?" Mzee Ajabu asked while washing and toweling his hands.

"About 100,000 bob."

"What? 100,000?" He paused. "Let me think about it," he said while getting up.

He walked to their master bedroom and entered his closet; everything seemed to be where he had left it. He put the code in his safe and opened it. He ran a hand on his head, wondering when he had put so much money in the safe. He smiled and closed it. He had a shower and jumped into bed, and in no time, he was snoring.

38.

Last Will & Testament

Mzee Ajabu walked into his office in high spirits. He looked at his daughter working at her desk, and a smile touched his face. The stars were finally starting to align, he thought. It was only a matter of time before everything fell into place. He sat behind his desk and dialed his CFO.

"Did we manage to get a 30-day payment policy on the accounts that have been pending for over a year?"

"We managed to get a 90-day policy, paid out in four quarters."

"That's a whole year. The least I expected was a 45-day payment policy over a six-month period?"

"Their cash flows are also stretched thin. It made more sense for them to take their business elsewhere than pay the amount in such a short duration of time."

"A 90-day payment policy for four quarters? How far will that set us back? Will we be forced to take another loan from the banks?"

"We should be okay if we don't stretch ourselves any further with miscellaneous expenditures."

"I hear you," Mzee Ajabu said, tapping his pen on his desk for a full minute. "Push them for a payment policy of 45 days over a six-month period for the first half of the debt, and they can have their 90-day payment period for the second half."

"I will get in touch with them immediately," the CFO said.

"Let's cross our fingers and hope they bite. In the meantime, wire 3.5 million Kenya shillings to my account. Put it under miscellaneous expenditures," Mzee Ajabu said and hung up.

After the transfer, he wired Helena three million shillings, then got into his M-pesa and sent his wife 30,000 bob. He picked up the handset of his office phone, leaned on his chair, and dialed his COO.

"Is everything ready to go in Rwanda and Uganda?" he asked.

"Everything is ready. We are set to open the branches this week."

"Good job, Kitana." He put the handset back on the receiver and swung on his chair. If only everybody worked as hard and as diligently as his Chief Operating Officer, things would run so much smoother. But then again, if wishes were horses beggars would ride, he thought and smiled.

He had one more important task on his in-tray. He had been putting off writing his last will and testament for a while, but he was now confident enough to write it. He opened a new Word document and placed his fingers on the keyboard.

'I have four children: Wairimu, Fred, Olivia, and Monica,' he began typing, but just before he could write the next sentence, his Kabambe started ringing. It was Helena; she was hysterical.

"Calm down, what's wrong…Monica overdosed on drugs…

Where is she...Okay, I'm sending help," Mzee Ajabu said and dialed Dr. Onyango.

After the call with their family doctor, he stared at his computer screen for a while, then placed his fingers on the keyboard, deleted the sentence he had written before, and started typing again.

<u>Last Will and Testament of Mzee Ajabu</u>

I, Mzee Ajabu, a citizen of Kenya and the CEO of Ajabu Digital, declare this to be my last will and testament and hereby revoke all wills made hereto by me, either jointly or severally.

i) I declare that I'm of legal age and of sound mind at the time of writing this will. This will expresses my wishes without undue influence or duress.

ii) I hereby declare that I am married to Mrs. Anne Ajabu, and my right-hand man is Mr. Patrick Kitana, hereby referred to as my COO.

iii) I hereby declare that I have the following children: Wairimu Ajabu, Fred Ajabu, and Olivia Ajabu.

iv) I hereby appoint my COO to be the executor of my will. In the event that my COO shall be unable to serve as an executor, I appoint my son, Fred Ajabu, as successor executor.

v) In the event of my death, my estate shall be divided equally among my children. My company structure shall be as follows. Olivia Ajabu shall serve as CHRO, Wairimu Ajabu as the COO under the condition that she passes her training, and my son, Fred Ajabu, shall serve as CEO.

Mzee Ajabu put the last full stop on the document and printed it. He did not know it by then, but immediately he finished writing his will, he condemned himself to an early grave. He signed and stamped it and sent a scanned copy to his lawyer. He made a photocopy for his home safe and put the original in his office safe, and a smile touched his face again. The stars were finally starting to align, he thought. It was only a matter of time before everything fell into place.

39.

Wairimu

WAIRIMU SAT NEXT to Chris at a restaurant near their office where they had just finished eating a meal of rice and chicken for lunch. She glanced at him. He was in blue khakis, black leather shoes, and a white shirt. She could tell he was well paid by the Subaru Outback keys on the table, the thin silver watch on his wrist, and his quiet and content manner.

She gazed into his brown eyes. He appeared to be in his late 20s. The yellow light in the restaurant bounced off his bald head, making it gleam. She used to say she would never date a short man, but looking at Chris, she was beginning to reconsider.

"You know I was told to stay away from you," she said playfully. She had just met him, but she felt as if they had known each other their entire life.

"You need to stop listening to Tatiana," he laughed. He had a vibrant laugh that gave Wairimu warmth.

"How many have you hit and then ran?" Wairimu giggled.

"Sometimes I think she's wasting her talents at the reception desk. She really should be running a gossip blog," Chris said and rubbed his beard in that content manner of his. "But enough about her—how are you finding the job so far?"

"I am managing. But do tell, what does a girl have to do around here to stop ferrying newspapers?"

"Those newspapers are really getting under your skin, huh?"

"Uh-huh."

"Things are about how you see them. If you see the glass as half-empty, you will never be able to enjoy what's inside it."

"What do you mean?"

"Sorry, I'm aging and beginning to sound like an old man. My meaning is, if you think your job is miserable, it will become the most miserable thing you have ever done."

"You're saying there is an advantage to ferrying newspapers?"

"Of course there is." He paused and ran a hand over his bald head. "You're not ferrying these newspapers to just any-one; you're ferrying them to the bigshots of the company. Spark a conversation and see where it goes."

"How? When half of them are barely in the office and the other half, well, they are dicks." Chris laughed, and butterflies fluttered in Wairimu's stomach. "Is the story about the HR lady true?" she leaned into him and whispered.

"You really need to stop listening to Tatiana," he said, his tone getting serious. "The head of HR, for example, compliment something that stands out about her every now and then: could be a watch or how she has done her makeup, and carry the con-versation from there. That is how you build valuable networks."

"You're not going to bill me for all this good advice, are you?"

"I'm in tech, not accounting, remember?" Chris smiled while getting into his wallet and settling the bill.

"Thank you. I will be sure to pay next time," Wairimu chimed.

"Who says there will be a next time?" They looked at each other and smiled. "We should get going," Chris added, looking at his watch and picking up his car keys.

"What's the hurry?"

"Okay, let's stay and give Tatiana something to gossip about."

Wairimu got up from her seat quickly, and they walked towards the office, giggling.

40.

Olivia

OLIVIA WAS SEATED on her bed. Her hair felt heavy on her head. She took her hairband and held it into a bun, but that did not help. She removed the hairband, and her hair fell on her face. She tucked it over her ears and opened her nightstand drawer, looking for scissors.

She got the scissors and started cutting it. She cut one tuft after another and stopped momentarily before dropping the scissors on the floor. She then buried her hand in her hair and pulled out a chunk of it.

Blood started trickling from her scalp, and then everything went dark.

"I thought we agreed it was going to be a boy?" Larry's voice boomed.

"I'm…sorry. I'm…sorry," Olivia stammered.

"What will I do with a girl? I can't kick a ball with her; I can't even watch the game with her."

"Forgive…me. I will do better next time."

"There isn't going to be a next time," Larry roared. He got a bag and started packing his clothes.

"Don't leave," Olivia pleaded.

She glanced at her daughter, sleeping in her crib. She looked every bit like him; it was uncanny. She went to her crib and started changing her, from the tiny dress she was wearing to trousers. "Look, Larry, I can make her become a boy. Please don't leave."

Larry finished packing his clothes and made for the door. Olivia got on her knees and grabbed one of his legs. "Please don't leave. He's a boy now, look." Larry wrenched free from her grip, hurried to the door, and banged it behind him. The next thing Olivia heard was the engine of his Subaru Impreza roaring and the sound receding and receding until it was quiet.

Olivia got up from the floor and went back to her daughter. She looked at her. She was giggling. She smiled and started changing her out of the trousers. There was a knock on the door before she was done. She picked her up and went with her to the door. Larry had come to his senses, she thought while turning the lock and opening the door.

Dr. Onyango stood on the other side of the door—holding the knife that she had been gifted by her mother during her baby shower. He lifted the knife and started stabbing her daughter with it: one time, two times, three times, countless times.

Olivia woke up screaming. She was on the floor next to the tufts of her hair and scissors, and her blood trickled from her scalp and hit the carpet with dripping sounds.

41.

Colors

FRED WOKE UP with a mind-numbing migraine. His lips were cracked and his throat was dry. He had not touched any drugs for a week, and it was driving him crazy. He got out of bed, had a shower, and put on the red uniform that had been provided for him in his room. The male nurse assigned to him inspected him to make sure he had bathed and gave him two pills and a glass of water.

There was a big round pill and a smaller oval one. Fred had heard chatter that the big one was for sedation and the smaller one was a detoxifier that helped with withdrawals. He swallowed the smaller one and hid the bigger one underneath his tongue. The male nurse inspected his mouth and escorted him to the dining hall.

Fred sat at his table with a glass of orange juice, two slices of bread, and two sausages. He looked around: nurses were standing strategically around the dining hall. He pretended to cough and dropped the big round pill into his hand and put it in his pocket. He glanced through the window and looked at the scenery. The rehab facility enjoyed picturesque views of greenery and rolling plains.

He shifted his gaze to the patients streaming into the hall for breakfast. They had different-colored uniforms: The majority were in blue, a few in gray, and even fewer in green and red. Fred looked at his red uniform and wondered what the colors meant as a chubby girl in a blue uniform came with her plate and sat next to him. She was light-skinned, with dark marks all over her arms.

"Hi, what's your redemption story?" she asked, and Fred got up and moved to another table.

His migraine had gotten worse; every bite of food was a struggle. Before he was halfway through, he got up, rushed to the toilet, and vomited everything he had eaten. He flushed the vomit together with the pill down the toilet bowl and rinsed his mouth. His nurse was waiting for him outside the toilet. He glanced at him and escorted him to his first session of the day.

They entered a small room that had four people seated in a circle: They were all in different-colored uniforms, except for the fourth one, who was the counselor—dressed in black pants and a crisp blue shirt. The nurse left after Fred was seated.

"Welcome, my name is Dr. Karani," he said. "We are going to go around, introduce ourselves, and share our redemption stories." He paused. There was a brown rod on the floor. He bent over and picked it up. "After you are done sharing your story, pass the rod to the next person," he said and passed it to a tall man on his right who was in gray uniform and who was missing all his front teeth.

"My name is Nick. I want to be clean for my family. I am tired of seeing them suffering because of me," he said and passed the rod to a short, fat man in a green uniform.

"My name is Bob. I'm doing this for my daughter. I'm tired of always being the one who is disappointing her," he said and passed it to a girl in a blue uniform. Fred looked at her and realized that she was the girl who sat next to him in the dining hall.

"My name is Monica. I am doing this for my well-being. I can no longer be the girl who lives in clubs and wakes up to different ceilings every other day." Her voice trembled as she passed the rod to Fred.

Fred took the rod and passed it to Dr. Karani. He did not listen to another word after that. The migraine started to make his head spin, and he dozed off. He woke up to an empty room with his nurse tapping him on the shoulder. It was time for his one-on-one session with his therapist.

He walked into his therapist's office and took a seat. His migraine had ebbed, but he still felt nauseated. He tried to suppress it by looking up—in his direct line of vision was a board with the uniform colors of the rehab facility and their meaning.

i)   Red Patients: Dysfunctional stage
ii)   Blue Patients: Acceptance stage
iii) Gray Patients: Recuperating stage
iv)   Green Patients: Discharge stage

Dr. Karani walked into the room and sat opposite Fed.

"Let's try this again," he said. "When did your drug problem begin?"

"I don't have a drug problem," Fred said expansively while swinging on his seat in his red uniform.

42.

Wairimu

BESIDES A PAYCHECK, Wairimu received something else at the end of the month: an email from HR that Kitana wanted to have a meeting with her in his office early the next morning.

She was a nervous wreck throughout the day. Kitana's assistant was being posted to Ajabu Digital's offices in Rwanda, and she suspected the meeting with Kitana would be an interview for her position.

She could not focus—her mind buzzed with a million things. When she realized she couldn't get any work done, she picked up her phone and texted Chris, asking him to meet her at the local restaurant for an early lunch.

She waited for him with a pen and a notebook. She saw him approaching her table and felt calmer. He looked elegant in his maroon shirt, brown pants, and brown leather shoes.

"A little bird told me you are getting ready for a big interview tomorrow," he said with a big smile on his face after sitting down and placing his car keys on the table.

"Was the little bird Tatiana?"

They laughed as the waitress came to take their orders. She ordered iced tea, and Chris ordered a Tusker Lite.

"Isn't it a bit early in the day to be drinking alcohol?"

"I'm sorry, Mom, I won't do it again," he teased.

"I guess it's five o'clock somewhere in the world," Wairimu said.

Chris leaned forward. "Tell me, what do you know about our COO, Mr. Kitana?"

"That he is business-like and cold."

"He is also immaculate. He wants you to know the answer before he asks the question."

Wairimu raised a brow and opened her notebook as the waitress brought their drinks and placed them on the table. "Enjoy," she said after opening Chris's Tusker Lite and then left their table.

Chris took a swig from his bottle and continued. "For example, when he asks you why you think you are the best person for the position, what are you going to tell him?"

"I'm going to tell him about my school grades."

Chris ran a hand over his scalp. "That's okay, but it's not enough. You need to tell him how smoothly you're running things in your current job. You need to tell him how you haven't received a single complaint since you took it up."

Wairimu took a sip from her iced tea and wrote in her notebook.

"I'm sure you have noticed some flaws in his assistant over the course of your job." Chris paused and took another swig from his Tusker Lite. "Point them out and tell him how you can fill those gaps."

Wairimu lifted her head from her notebook. "How should

I negotiate a salary bump?" she asked after taking another sip from her iced tea.

"Tell him the current market rate and arrive at a middle ground with him based on what you can deliver."

Wairimu lifted her head from her notebook. "Is there anything else I should know?"

"That's pretty much it."

She lifted her hand in the air and Chris high-fived it.

"Thank you, Mr. Womanizer," she said, and they both laughed.

Chris drank the last dregs of his Tusker Lite. "I need to run; I have a team meeting in an hour." He got into his pocket and popped a mint into his mouth. He put the packet of mints back into his pocket and came out with his wallet.

"No, no, no. This one's on me."

"Are you sure?"

Wairimu nodded.

"Okay, wishing you success." Chris picked his car keys and lifted his hand, and they high-fived again. "Tell me how it goes."

Wairimu sat at the table, sipping her iced tea while reading through her notes. She decided she wouldn't go back to the office; she would clock out early so that she could have enough time to go shopping and prepare for the interview.

43.

Mrs. Ajabu

AFTER MZEE AJABU left in the morning, Mrs. Ajabu went to their master bedroom and opened his safe: It was a habit she had started after she got its codes. The money she had put was still there, but there was a new document. Her husband's last will and testament. She looked at it and a smile almost touched her face before she put it back. She locked the safe and went to the kitchen.

She was visiting her son in Nanyuki, and she wanted to prepare his favorite food. She opened the small fridge and poured herself a large glass of wine before she started cooking.

Fred's behavior was weighing heavy on her heart. The rehabilitation facility had called her and told her Fred was not cooperating.

Wairimu was working, and Olivia's problem had been fixed. How was it that her favorite child was the one who was struggling? she wondered while taking a gulp from her wine glass.

She put down the glass, turned on the burner, and started

frying chicken wings. She turned on another burner and started making *chapatis* while the chicken cooked. She turned off the burners after she was done and started making a bowl of fruit salad.

She was slicing watermelon when Olivia walked into the kitchen. She was wearing a baggy t-shirt and baggy trousers, and her head was wrapped with a headband.

"Kamom, I have made *chapos*. Will you have them with tea?" Mrs. Ajabu asked.

Olivia stared at her with vacant eyes and left the kitchen.

Mrs. Ajabu reached for her wine glass, emptied it, and got back to slicing the watermelon. She cut it into small pieces and mixed it with the already diced bananas, pawpaws, and pineapples. She packed the food into hotpots and the fruit salad into a lunchbox. She put everything into a *kiondoo* and took it to the sitting room.

She found Olivia seated on the couch, staring at the rotating fan and listening to the clinking sounds of the crystals on the chandelier. She placed the *kiondoo* on the table, went back to the kitchen, and fixed her a plate of *chapatis* and chicken wings.

"Eat something, Kamom," she said while placing the plate next to her and going to their master bedroom. Olivia glanced at the plate, then went back to staring at the ceiling.

Mrs. Ajabu took a shower and had a change of clothes. She came back to find Olivia's eyes fixated on the rotating fan and the chandelier, her food untouched.

She went to the kitchen and poured herself another large glass of wine. *She will snap out of it soon,* she convinced herself while taking a gulp. She emptied the glass, dialed a taxi, picked up her *kiondoo,* and left the house.

She went back hurriedly and nudged Olivia out of her stupor. "What will people say if they find you here?" she asked while helping her to her bedroom before leaving the house again.

Her heart was heavy as she sat inside the taxi headed for the rehabilitation facility in Nanyuki. Wairimu was working, and Olivia's problem had been fixed. How was it that her favorite child was the one that was struggling? She leaned into her seat. She would fix Fred's problems today, she decided and felt the weight on her heart ease.

44.

Promotion

WAIRIMU WAS IN a figure-hugging black dress that cut slightly above her knees, black strap heels, and was carrying a gray clutch bag. She had spent almost half of her salary to pull off the look. It would all be worth it, she told herself as she pushed the door and entered the COO's office.

Mr. Kitana was seated behind his desk, clacking away at his Macbook. "Have a seat. I will be with you shortly," he said and buried his face in his laptop. Wairimu took a seat at the small meeting table in the middle of his office and crossed her legs. Her dress rolled up her thighs a few inches. She pulled it down, opened her notebook, and started going through her notes.

Kitana got up from his desk, picked his iPad, and walked towards Wairimu. He was in a blue suit, black shoes, and a thin gold watch. The citrus in his scent stained Wairimu's nose as he took a seat next to her.

"Good morning," he said while crossing his legs and facing

Wairimu.

"Good morning," Wairimu replied, not knowing what to do with herself now.

"This will be a short meeting." Kitana tapped on his iPad. "How are you finding your job so far?"

Wairimu wondered if this was the part where she told him how smoothly she was running things and how she hadn't received a single complaint from anyone since she started.

"It's been okay so far," she said while uncrossing her legs. Her dress rolled up again, and she pulled it down.

"How are the colleagues treating you?"

"They have been great."

"Glad to hear it," Kitana said while placing his iPad on the table. "The reason I called you this morning is because there has been a development." He paused as Wairimu straightened up on her seat.

"What development?" she asked.

"Our receptionist, Tatiana, is going on maternity leave, and we want you to hold her position."

Wairimu's jaw tightened. "What about...the newspapers and...inventory...management?" she stammered.

"You will handle that too."

"Will there be a salary bump?"

"Not exactly. You have been here for barely a month."

Wairimu nodded while clenching her teeth. Beads of sweat had formed on her forehead.

"Thank you for your time, Miss Wairimu," Kitana said while picking up his iPad from the table. "HR will set you up." He uncrossed his legs and got up, his perfume staining Wairimu's nose again. "If there is nothing else, that will be all," he added.

"Thank...you," she stammered while getting up. She went to pick up her notebook, and it fell on the floor. She bent over to pick it as Kitana was walking to his desk.

"One more thing, Wairimu," Kitana said after she stood up. "Don't be clocking out early when you haven't gotten permission."

Wairimu had the urge to snatch his iPad and smack him with it. "That is understood," she said and walked out of his office with her chin up.

45.

Olivia

AFTER HER MOM left the house, Olivia got up from her bed and went to the bathroom. She opened the faucet and let the water run over her body. She stood there as it soaked her clothes. She listened to the sound of it running, and then it got quiet, and everything went dark.

She opened her eyes and watched her daughter running to class. It was her first day in school, and she was thrilled. "Gakenia, Gakenia," she called out. She had named her Gakenia because she had brought joy into her life.

Gakenia came running, with a big smile on her face.

"You have forgotten your lunchbox," Olivia said.

"Thank you, Mom. I love you," Gakenia said while picking up the lunchbox.

"I love you too," Olivia said and kissed her on the forehead.

"See you after school, Mom," she said and ran to her class.

Olivia saw her disappear behind the door and felt loneliness consume her. She decided to follow her daughter to class and keep her company.

She pushed open the door and entered the class. It was full of kids, and the teacher was her mother. She moved her gaze around the class, but she could not spot her daughter.

"Where is she?" she asked her mother.

"Where is who?"

"Gakenia."

"Who is that?"

"My daughter, Gakenia. You know her. You know her!" she shouted.

A student in the class stood up. Olivia turned to look at her. She had Wairimu's face. "I saw her getting out of the class with another man," she said and sat down.

Olivia stormed out of the class and started running while shouting Gakenia's name. She got to the gate and saw her with the man. *Larry finally got back to his senses and came back for us,* Olivia thought while running towards them.

She got closer to them, and the man turned around. It was Dr. Onyango. "Give my daughter back!" she shouted, still running towards them. It was strange; the more she ran after them, the further away they got from her.

"Gakenia!" she shouted as they disappeared into the horizon. "Gakenia!" She opened her eyes, screaming. She was back in the bathroom, with the water running on her body and soaking her clothes.

46.

Fred

Fred sat in the dining hall for lunch with a plate of mashed potatoes, cabbage, and beef stew after his counseling session. "I don't have a drug problem," he said to himself. His migraine throbbed at his temples, and he felt as if there was a fire lit in his throat. The only silver lining was that he had vomited only half of his breakfast in the morning instead of all of it—and his mother was visiting him later in the afternoon.

"Hi, what's your name?" It was Monica, the chubby light-skinned girl sitting at his table again. "You know, acceptance is the first step to recovery," she continued.

Fred took his plate and moved to another table. He struggled through his food until he was halfway done. He lifted his spoon to take another bite, and his male nurse rushed towards him and stopped him. He got up and followed him to the office block where he had been assigned to be cleaning.

The rehabilitation facility was self-sufficient. Every patient besides the ones that were in critical condition had duties. There were those who cleaned floors and dusted, those who did laundry, and those who did the cooking. Fred dragged his feet while carrying a bucket and a mop to the office block and found Nick and Bob chattering while cutting the grass next to the verandah.

"I snorted powder in Nairobi, and I woke up in the Aberdare Ranges with only my underwear," Bob was saying, and Nick laughed, exposing his missing teeth. Fred drained the water from his mop and started cleaning the verandah—all the while, his migraine throbbed and he fought to keep his lunch in his stomach. The only thing that was keeping him standing was the visitation from his mom later in the day, he realized.

"I was a dealer," Nick was saying. "You see my missing front teeth—my addiction had gotten so bad that I had sold everything I could sell to feed it, and after there was nothing left, I started using the drugs I was meant to sell. My boss found out and told me since I had nothing he could sell, he would sell my teeth instead, and that's how I lost all my incisors."

Fred looked at him and wondered if he could give him his boss's contacts. He needed a hit badly. "What about you?" Someone was directing their voice towards Fred. He didn't know who it was between Bob and Nick, nor did he care. He was reminiscing on how it felt to have drugs swimming in his veins and being lifted off like a rocket to another world.

He was shaken out of his stupor by the voice of his nurse telling him he had missed a spot.

After he was done, he returned the cleaning equipment to the store and went to the TV room. There were various activities that patients could do after chores: sports, arts and crafts, or volunteering at a nearby children's home. Fred chose to watch *National Geographic* instead.

He sat in the TV room alone and stared at the screen. He watched a gazelle escape from the jaws of a lion while his migraine throbbed, and he fought to keep his lunch in his stomach and waited for the intercom to call his name when his mom arrived.

47.

Mrs. Ajabu

Mrs. Ajabu laid a *leso* on the field and sat down with her son. She looked at him. He was a shadow of what he used to look like. He had lost weight, his lips were cracked, and he looked anxious. She got a bottle of Vaseline from her handbag, opened it, and smeared some of it on his lips.

"How are you finding this place, son," she asked while removing hotpots from her *kiondoo* and placing them on the *leso*.

"It sucks, Mom. They are giving me pills that are not helping me and making me scrub floors. Let's go home, Mom," he complained.

Mrs. Ajabu got a plate and served him *chapatis* and chicken wings. Immediately he took a bite, he vomited the entire meal of mashed potatoes, cabbage, and beef stew he had eaten earlier—all over the grass and on his plate.

They got up and moved to another section of the field. Mrs. Ajabu got a bottle of water from his bag, wetted a handkerchief, and dabbed her son's forehead with it. "Don't worry, you'll get better," she said while using the handkerchief to clean his mouth and handing him the bottle of water to drink.

"You need to follow the program, Fred," Mrs. Ajabu said, finding it difficult to tell her son what he did not want to hear for the first time in a long time. "You need to take all the drugs they are giving you and accept you have a problem so you can get well," she said while fixing him another plate.

"Why should I get better? My life sucks anyway," Fred said and started sobbing.

Mrs. Ajabu held him and used her blouse to wipe his tears.

"Your father has named you the successor to his company," she said with a more serious tone than the mothering one she had been using. "What do you think he will do when he realizes you are a drug addict who complains about simple chores and taking medicine that is good for you?"

Fred broke away from his mother's embrace. "He has named me the successor of his company?" he asked, surprised. He wiped the tears from his eyes with the back of his hand and bit a chicken wing.

"Do you now realize why you need to get your act together?"

"I don't know anything about running a company, Mom."

"You will be a far much better CEO than he is. You will bring the money home instead of taking it to whores as he does."

Fred nodded in shock. He was seeing a completely different side of his mom now.

"You know you have been confined to your room for so long you don't even know how your father lives. Come close; let me show you something."

Mrs. Ajabu opened her phone's photo gallery and showed him pictures of his father's office, his helicopter, his private jet, and the yacht in their beach house in Mombasa.

"Do you want all this to go to your elder sister?"

Fred nodded his head sideways.

"That's what will happen if you don't get it together."

"I will follow the program, starting today, I promise."

"Good, after that, we can move to the next step."

"What is that?"

"A coup. You need to take your father's company sooner rather than later."

Fred nodded with a toothy grin and wiped his plate of food and bowl of fruit salad clean.

He told his mom stories about Nick, Bob, Monica, Dr. Karani, and the male nurse assigned to him. Mrs. Ajabu laughed when he told her about Monica. "Be nice to her. You can never have too many friends in a place like this," she said.

They wrapped up, and Mrs. Ajabu bid her son goodbye. On the taxi drive back to Nairobi, her heart was lighter. Wairimu was working, Olivia's problem had been fixed, and she had corrected the course of Fred's life. It was now just a matter of time before she started living how she had been meant to live. *Like a queen,* she thought and grinned.

48.

Golf

Mzee Ajabu was in a mood as he walked into Muthaiga Country Club. He was having a difficult time stomaching the fact that he had built a multi-billion-shilling company, yet he was getting ready to kiss ass. It was necessary if he was going to fix the cash flow problems that were threatening to collapse the very giant he had built, he reminded himself.

He stretched his waist and asked his caddie to hand him the pitching wedge. He stretched some more and rubbed his *kitambi* before placing the golf ball on the tee and aiming at it with his pitching wedge. Then, with a fine swing of his hips, he hit the ball. It did not go very far. It rolled and tapered off into one of the bunkers nearby.

Mzee Ajabu groaned. He loathed the game of golf, maybe even more than kissing ass. He remembered a time when what you had done spoke for itself. That was a forgotten art, he decided while bending his back, swinging his hips, and hitting the ball again—but that was also duff.

"You're losing your touch," a voice boomed from behind. It was Tom, the Chief Executive Officer of Kenya Independent Bank—the biggest bank in the country. Tom stood 6'1, early 40s, dark of complexion, and sharp of brains. He was the man who was in a position to solve Mzee Ajabu's cash flow problems.

"Slippery pitching wedge," Mzee Ajabu defended himself, embarrassed.

"It is a bad workman who quarrels with his tools," Tom said, and they both laughed.

They glanced at each other after embracing. They were both men who knew what it took to get to the top. They were also men who understood the dance. There were no free lunches; there was only giving and taking. The question was ever: who would be doing the giving and who the taking?

"Tom, even the grass looks greener now that you are here," Mzee Ajabu said.

"You flatter me. How are your wife and kids?"

"My wife is okay, the kids too." He paused and rubbed his *kitambi*. "Wairimu was giving us trouble, but she's turning around."

"That one is a fireball, my friend. If I was not so old, we could have discussed dowry." Tom had two wives, so Mzee Ajabu knew the statement was not too far-fetched. He laughed nervously, realizing that he was losing the rhetoric battle. "But you know what they say, the apple doesn't fall far from the tree," Tom said expansively.

Mzee Ajabu coughed as if something had caught in his throat.

"Shall we begin?" Tom asked.

"Of course," Mzee Ajabu managed to mouth after clearing his windpipe.

Tom's caddie handed him the 7-iron golf club. He steadied the ball on the tee and took a fine swing. It flew into the air and out of sight. There was a reason he had a handicap of zero.

Mzee Ajabu's jaw tightened as he placed the golf ball on the tee and aimed at it with his pitching wedge. He swung his hips with vigor and missed the ball by a mile—almost taking to the ground. He steadied himself and took another swing. The ball tapered off and fell into a nearby pond. He looked at Tom, wearing a look of embarrassment.

"You're right; I'm losing my touch," he said. "But do tell, what do I need to do to get your bank to stand as a buffer for Ajabu Digital?"

Tom steadied another golf ball on the tee and took another fine swing. "My friend, you know I'm a straight shooter," he began. "I pitched your idea to the board. They feel you're swimming in deep waters. You're in how many countries now: Kenya, Uganda, Botswana...?"

"Rwanda," Mzee Ajabu corrected him.

"Yes, Rwanda. I keep forgetting that one. The long and short of it is, you're high-risk, and you know we bankers are risk-averse."

"There is no way you can go around it?" he asked.

Tom steadied himself and swung his hips to mimic Mzee Ajabu and took another swing.

"You could go public, you know."

Mzee Ajabu frowned. He could not risk going public, not when he had seen too many founders and their families left in the cold by a mercenary board of directors; and who was to say Tom wasn't looking to buy the majority of the shares? They were all sharks here, and he knew Tom could smell blood.

"Come into my office at the Mirage and let's talk about this over a cup of tea with air conditioning," Mzee Ajabu said after realizing he couldn't get through to the man today unless he offered him a board seat or his daughter, Wairimu.

"I will open up a day, but no promises," Tom said after they embraced.

Mzee Ajabu summoned his caddie and got into the golf cart. As he was driven towards the clubhouse, he realized he was exhausted—less by the game and more from not getting what he wanted. He reached into his pocket and fished out his phone. He could use another relaxing trip, he thought while dialing Diana.

49.

Wairimu

WAIRIMU'S MORNING WAS busy with angry suppliers whose payments were overdue. They were seated in the lounge area of the reception desk, and whenever one left, another one came in.

"Hello, how can I help you?" Wairimu asked after the third one in line got up from the lounge area and walked up to her desk.

"My name is Mutiso. I'm here to inquire about my delayed payment. I supply branded merchandise for Ajabu Digital," a smartly dressed man said while supporting his weight on the reception desk.

"Give me a minute, Mutiso," Wairimu said while dialing the debtor's department. "Your check is ready, but the final signatory is away. Please check back next week," she said and flashed him a smile while putting the handset back on the receiver. The man hesitated, then turned back and headed for the exit.

"My name is Sonia. I'm here about my check," a woman

wearing horn-rimmed glasses was saying. "I worked on an acti-vation campaign for Ajabu Digital six months ago," she added.

"Give me a second, Sonia," Wairimu said and dialed the debtor's department again. "Your check is ready, but the final sig-natory is away. Please check back next week," she repeated her-self with a smile. She was smiling falsely so often now, she was afraid her face would crack.

"Your check is ready, but the final signatory is away. Please check back next week," she was saying to the fifth supplier after pretending to dial the debtor's department.

"I haven't paid my rent, my electricity bill, my water bill, all because Ajabu Digital can't hold up their end of the contract. Urgh!" the supplier said and stormed out.

"Hello, how can I help you?" Wairimu asked the sixth supplier in line.

***

It was around 9:00 am when the newspapers arrived. She re-quested the suppliers to be patient and bent over the stack of newspapers. The flowy skirt she was wearing climbed up and exposed the back of her thighs. She had asked her supervisor, the new Assistant COO, if she could wear trousers, but she had refused, insisting that she needed to look the part.

She called the tea lady to stand in for her and headed for the first floor in her flowy red skirt, purple heels, and blouse.

She was beginning to understand why their chief of staff was ever in a mood. She was grappling with turnover prob-lems and was always on the phone with her subordinates, going through recruitment strategies and on her MacBook, reviewing performance. Some days Wairimu felt her job was harder than hers.

After giving her her papers, she went to the acquisition and research offices. The managers were both absent. She folded their newspapers in half, placed them on their desks, and left for the fifth floor.

The creative and the social media departments were a ghost town as usual at these hours of the morning. She sometimes wondered how things got done on this side at all. She placed the account directors' and social media managers' newspapers on their desks, closed their office doors behind her, and walked to the creative directors' offices.

She did the same thing, except for the last office, which was occupied. "Come in," a voice said after she knocked. There was a lean, dark guy with a mohawk on his head eyeballing an iMac.

After Wairimu had folded his newspapers in half and placed them on his desk, he got up from his desk and started scribbling something with a blue marker on a portable whiteboard.

"What is that about?" she asked curiously.

"This is a storyboard. A new idea we are pitching to a client."

She found it fascinating that he was in a business that sold ideas.

"How do you arrive at these ideas?"

"It's all very boring," he said after running a hand through his mohawk. "We get a brief from the client, then have a creative brainstorm. We crank up the music and drink alcohol while bouncing ideas off each other. Then we go with the one that sucks the least—you should attend one," he added.

"I don't drink alcohol," Wairimu said defensively.

"Well, there is always a first." He grinned. "The name is Winfred, by the way."

"I'm Wairimu," she said and started leaving before turning back just when she was at the door. "I will stop by when I find someone to hold the reception desk long enough that I'm not fired." Winfred smiled and went back to his storyboard, and

Wairimu faded to the IT department on the seventh floor.

She gave all the tech honchos their newspapers and turned the lock on Chris's office to find him behind his desk. She handed him his newspapers, and he unfolded them. He opened the *Daily Nation* from the back and started filling the crossword puzzle.

"I heard about the interview. How are you holding up?" he asked with his head bent over the newspaper.

"I'm over it," Wairimu said with a flat tone.

"Some we lose, some we win," Chris said, lifting his head from the newspaper.

"It's okay. I guess it's like you said. I should start looking at the glass as half-full," she said and started walking toward the door.

"Let me get that for you," Chris got up and opened the door for her. "Lunch today?" he asked while holding the door.

"Sure."

"This time it's my treat," he added.

Wairimu smiled and dissolved to the ninth floor. Her smile was wiped off her face when she saw the number of people waiting in the reception lounge area for her to attend to them.

50.

Mood Swings

FRED WOKE UP in the morning with a headache, nausea, and a scratchy throat. He had a shower and changed into his red uniform. His nurse inspected him before handing him his pills and a glass of water. He put both the round and oval one in his mouth and washed them down with the water.

He walked with the nurse to the dining hall. He was starting to realize that only patients in red were guarded closely by their nurses. Even this was temporary, he thought. He would improve and work his way through blue, gray, and green uniforms in no time at all.

He sat in the dining hall with a cup of porridge, a banana, and three slices of oatmeal bread and wondered how differently he would run his father's company. Then he realized he did not know the first thing about running a company besides spending the money it produced. Images of weed and powder flashed in his mind and exacerbated his headache.

He was peeling his banana while wondering if eating it would make his nausea worse when a shadow blocked his light. It was Monica. She sat down with her tray across from him.

"Hi, what's your name," she chirped after taking a sip from her porridge.

Fred stayed quiet for what felt like a minute. He finished peeling his banana and took a bite. "I'm Fred," he said after swallowing.

"What's your redemption story?" she asked while peeling her banana.

"I don't have one. I just want to get my green uniform and get the hell out of here." They both stayed silent for a while, taking sips from their porridge and chewing their oatmeal bread.

"How did you get your blue uniform?" Fred broke the silence.

"I don't know. I just woke up one day and found it in my room," Monica said.

Fred looked at her, disappointed with her answer, and took another bite of his banana.

"It's not one thing. That's for sure," she said, trying to make up for it.

"Then what is it?" Fred asked, his tone rising and his headache turning into a migraine.

"I guess it's a bit of everything."

"You don't want to tell me the truth, do you? You want me to be stuck here with you for the rest of my life, eh?" Fred was shouting now.

His nurse interrupted them and asked if everything was okay. Fred responded by saying everything was fine, and his nurse lifted him from the table and told him it was time for his morning counseling session. They walked towards the session with his head throbbing, his throat scratchy, and his stomach uneasy. He knew he wouldn't be getting a blue uniform that day.

51.

Diana

Mzee Ajabu's Bell 206 helicopter took off at Wilson Airport. He was on board with his pilot—who also doubled as the captain of his yacht—and Diana. She took a selfie of herself in the cabin with two fingers in the air. *Mombasa getaway. #HelicopterLife,* she captioned it and shared it on her Instagram stories.

Within the hour, the chopper was landing on a helipad on Mzee Ajabu's beach house in Mombasa, which was more of a restaurant than a house because it had a fully functioning staff made of a chef, a sous chef, and four servants.

The first thing Mzee Ajabu did when he landed was call his wife. "I'm picking up some business partners in Mombasa. I won't be around for the weekend," he said and hung up.

The first thing Diana did when she landed was change into her peach-colored bathing suit and pose this way and that while one of the beach house's servants took photos of her on the shoreline. *Queen of the beach,* she captioned one of the photos and posted it on her Instagram profile.

The second thing she did was go into the master bedroom and turn the faucet to fill the bathtub with warm water. Mzee Ajabu entered the tub, and she began lathering his whole body with soap. "You missed a spot," Mzee Ajabu said while lifting his buttocks.

After she was done, she rinsed, toweled, oiled, and massaged him. She dressed him in white trousers and a white t-shirt before dressing herself in a yellow maxi dress, and they headed to his yacht, Sunseeker, for dinner.

It was not the first time Diana was inside Mzee Ajabu's yacht, but her heart skipped a beat every time she was on board the Sunseeker. It had three decks: the lower deck, the main deck, and the sun deck. The lower deck had four en suite guest accommodations. The main deck had a galley, lounge and dining area, and an en suite master cabin, complete with a king-size bed and a walk-in closet.

The yacht was a cash pit, and it needed money every month for repairs, crew salaries, insurance, dock fees, and fuel, but Mzee Ajabu never once thought of getting rid of it.

Diana climbed up the stairs to the sun deck, which had a cocktail bar and a lounge area, complete with a Jacuzzi. She handed her phone to one of the crew members, and she posed this way and that next to the Jacuzzi as they cruised through the Indian Ocean, which was illuminated by the moonlight. *Not all stars belong to the sky. #YachtLife,* she captioned one of the photos and posted it on her Instagram profile.

They sat down at the dining area on the main deck. Diana had prawns with a glass of champagne, while Mzee Ajabu had *ugali,* and pan-fried liver and onions with a glass of water. Diana took her phone and snapped a picture of her meal. *Eating like royalty. Boss Babe Vibes,* she captioned the photo and shared it on her

Instagram stories.

After dinner, they retired to the master cabin. Mzee Ajabu unbuckled his white trousers and took Diana from the back with her yellow maxi dress on. He did not pump for two minutes before he climaxed. Diana held him in the baby position she often held him in and hummed a lullaby to him until he fell asleep. She did not care to capture the moment and share it on her Instagram account.

52.

Creative Brainstorm

WINFRED HAD PUSHED the creative brainstorm to after working hours, and that was how Wairimu found herself in the lounge area of the creative department, surrounded by creative types dressed in colorful clothes, chattering, smoking, drinking, and shooting pool.

This is madness, she thought as she settled down on one of the sofas next to Winfred.

"Wairimu, meet the gang," Winfred started talking, and everyone in the lounge quieted. "Across from you is Jackeline—she's the community manager for the brand—and the guys at the pool table are Ryan, the brand's account manager, and Samuel, the brand's copywriter," he pointed. "Gang, Wairimu," he added.

"Karibu," they sang in unison.

Winfred ran a hand through his mohawk and scribbled 'Mambo Tele Creative Brainstorm' on his portable whiteboard with his blue marker. "Mambo Tele maize flour is trying to appeal to the everyday person." He cleared his voice. "It's a pioneer of maize flour, but cheaper alternatives are undercutting it. Our job is to make that stop," he said finally.

"If they won't lower their prices, why not make it a luxury flour? There is a reason you pay 20 bob for *ugali* at your local *kibanda* and 1,000 bob for the same *ugali* at a five-star hotel. We could have high-end influencers enjoying a hearty meal with the flour," Samuel said while aiming at the white ball with his cue stick. The light in the lounge caught his nose ring, and it gleamed.

"That's a good idea," Winfred responded while scribbling 'Kibanda' on his whiteboard. "The only problem is, there is already a luxury maize flour. We might solve one problem and step right into another one."

"Even if the price is steep, *ugali* is still a mass product," Jackeline said, taking a pull from her cigarette and blowing a cloud of smoke through her nostrils as a beaded Maasai necklace danced on her neck.

Winfred ran a hand through his mohawk again and scribbled the words, 'Mass product' on his whiteboard.

"Why don't we do a film with an ordinary family, preferably in *mashambani,* enjoying the maize flour? Perhaps we can use our local celebrities for appeal," Ryan said while taking a swig from a bottle of Tusker. He was tall, with a technicolor scarf around his neck. He resembled a celebrity himself, Wairimu thought.

"Let's put a pin on that. Wairimu, anything?" Winfred asked while shifting his gaze to her.

Wairimu stirred out of her thoughts and straightened up. "I think the question we should be asking ourselves is, where do most people enjoy *ugali?*" she began. "I mean, sure, they enjoy it at home, but the major places people partake in it are butcheries, restaurants—Sam has mentioned *vibanda*..." She glanced at him momentarily. "Why can't we partner with some of these joints?

Anybody eating beef, fish, pork, or anything that needs *ugali* as an accompaniment, should be eating it with Mambo Tele maize flour."

The lounge area had gone pin-drop silent.

"And the question of having inferior brands undercutting us—why not have ads out saying something like, 'Mambo Tele, the only maize flour,' or something of the sort to make them look like pretenders and ultimately irrelevant?"

The room was uproarious.

"Give her one on the house," Ryan chanted, raising his bottle of beer.

That's the direction the strategy took, and that was the idea that was adopted for the campaign.

53.

Mrs. Ajabu

Mrs. Ajabu watched her husband walk into the house and take a seat next to her and felt resentment froth up in her mouth.

"Will you eat supper?" she asked him.

"Wait a minute, let me catch my breath first," he groaned while rubbing his *kitambi.*

Mrs. Ajabu glanced at him again. He looked relaxed, and he had sunburns across his neck. She looked away, wondering what kind of business meeting he had had that had given him sunburns. Her jaw tightened, and she craved a glass of wine when she realized she knew the answer.

She distracted herself with thoughts of her recuperating son. She had visited him recently, and he was taking his medication, listening to his counselors, and getting better. It wouldn't be long now until he was healthy and strong enough to take up the mantle, and for her husband to pay for all those days he short-changed her and left her in the cold.

"Is that Olivia? I haven't seen her in a while," Mzee Ajabu was saying, and Mrs. Ajabu was stirred out of her thoughts.

Olivia was sprawled on the couch, sound asleep, with a blanket covering her. Mrs. Ajabu had moved her from the bedroom because her husband had been asking about her, and she didn't want him to raise an alarm.

"Yes," Mrs. Ajabu responded. "She's exhausted. She's just from her driving classes in town," she added.

"Has she decided what course she will take in campus?"

"Human Resource Management, I think."

"That's my girl. She's going to be my chief of staff," Mzee Ajabu said while getting up from his seat and smooching her on the forehead. "I'm being told by my staff that Wairimu is doing fantastic at the office, but I haven't heard from Fred in a while?" he asked, taking his seat.

"Fred is still in his finance seminar, though it's coming to an end. It was running for about three months, I think," Mrs. Ajabu said flatly.

"Three months," Mzee Ajabu said while removing his coat. "He better come back a business genius. Ajabu Digital could use his skills in solving a few problems."

"There is also the matter of his graduation party?" Mrs. Ajabu said nonchalantly.

"I will see what I can do." Mzee Ajabu paused. "What have you cooked?" he asked, changing the subject.

"*Matoke* and fried meat."

"*Matoke*, again? I will have it for breakfast tomorrow," he said, picked up his coat, and went to their master bedroom.

Mrs. Ajabu's resentment frothed up her mouth again after he left. She thought of having a glass of wine but decided against it. She distracted herself by looking at Olivia. She looked fickle, even covered by that blanket. *I saved her. She will thank me someday,* she reminded herself.

She turned her thoughts to Fred. It wouldn't be long now until he was healthy and strong enough to take up his father's mantle. It wouldn't be long now until her plan hatched.

54.

Climbing the Ranks?

KITANA CALLED WAIRIMU to his office. Her heart was in her mouth as she turned the lock and pushed open the door. *What position had opened up this time, the tea lady's?* she wondered nervously.

"Have a seat," Kitana said while getting up from his desk.

Wairimu smoothed her gray dress from behind and took a seat at the small meeting table. Kitana joined her. His scent burned her nose, and she felt light-headed for a split second.

She glanced at him. He looked calm, but then he always looked calm. Wairimu was quickly realizing that he was one of those people with an impassive face that you couldn't read.

"How are you finding the job?" he asked after sitting down.

"It's tough."

"Well, that's the thing with anything of value—it's difficult."

Wairimu looked at him and, for the first time, realized he was looking out for her best interests. She smoothed her dress and sat up straight.

"How come we owe all these people money? What's up with that?" she asked.

"We have cash flow problems; your father has been trying to sort it out," Kitana replied, impressed by her observation.

"Cash flow problems?"

"Yes, Ajabu Digital is expanding too fast. We have a lot of business, and with a lot of business comes many suppliers, employees, and miscellaneous bills. Our cash reserves are almost always stretched."

"Is there a solution?"

"The quickest one would be going public. Having the citizenry buy our shares en-masse would fix our cash flow problems for sure."

"But we won't do it, will we?"

"Well, your dad has always been a stickler about keeping the business in the family. He doesn't want to lose control to shareholders, and in his words, he doesn't want to lose the company culture."

Wairimu wondered what company culture that was. High-stress levels and lopsided decision-making? She did not finish musing before Kitana interrupted.

"The next and best alternative is to have a big bank bet on us and increase our cash reserves. Your dad has been pushing with Kenya International Bank, but Tom, the CEO, won't fold. I think it's a play to force your dad to go public, then he can swoop in and buy a majority of the shares and consequently own the biggest advertising agency in the country.

Wairimu moved on her chair to get comfortable. She had read about cash flow wrangles in her project management classes, but she had never thought they would hit so close to home.

"If there is any way I can help...uhmm, I'm prepared to burn the midnight oil," she said.

"It's being handled." Kitana paused. "The reason I called you here was because we want to move you."

Wairimu held on to her seat and got ready.

"You have been fantastic with the newspapers, inventory, and as a receptionist. Winfred also told me your brilliant input in their creative brainstorm," Kitana added.

Mzee Ajabu's direction had been to keep Wairimu doing leg work for a year, but after a few months on the job, Kitana realized she was sharper than he had given her credit for. She was learning fast and executing her duties more efficiently than people that had been there for years.

"We are going to give you an account to direct," Wairimu heard him say, and her mouth formed an 'O' in disbelief. "You are going to handle Mambo Tele maize flour. And you will have a team of three—I think you have already met Jackeline, Sam, and Ryan?"

Wairimu nodded.

"We will put you on probation for three months and discuss a salary increase then."

Wairimu nodded again, still in disbelief.

"You can finish your duties today and hand-over to Tatiana. She will be back tomorrow; I hope you have missed her," he added.

Wairimu thought of Tatiana and smiled nervously. She could already hear the gossip of her climbing the ranks faster than she should have, and she wasn't looking forward to it.

"You start tomorrow on the fifth floor. You will report directly to me. You will also work very closely with Winfred, the creative director. He spoke very highly of you," Kitana said finally.

Wairimu was at a loss for words. "Thank you," she said, still surprised.

"Wishing you the best of luck," Kitana said while getting up. "Even though I know you won't need it."

Wairimu got up, and they shook hands.

For the first time, she felt she could shake things up. She decided to do a bit of shopping after work. She started opening the door and turned before stepping out.

"Can I clock out early today? I need to…"

"Sure," Kitana said, taking a seat behind his desk.

Wairimu turned the lock and got out of his office, tasting the title 'Account Director' in her mouth and deciding she loved the flavor of it.

55.

Growth

FRED WAS STARTING to understand what Monica had meant when she said that it was not one thing that got you a different-colored set of uniforms. It was an increment of many different things. It was how you took care of your hygiene, how you related with others, how you opened up, and how you executed your chores.

He dried his duster and started washing the office block verandah. His headache was mild, and his nausea had receded. Since he started taking both of his pills, he noticed he was getting better. His lips were no longer as cracked, and his throat was less scratchy.

He left his bucket and duster on the verandah, went to the facilities store, and came back with a scrubbing brush. He got on his knees and started scrubbing the floor. Nick and Bob were now both in green uniform. They were landscaping the plants next to the office block while chattering and laughing.

"What is the first thing you will do when you get out of

here?" Bob was asking Nick.

Nick humped the bougainvillea, and they both broke into a laugh. "What about you," Nick asked.

"Spend time with my daughter," Bob said.

"Aww, that's so cute," Nick said, and they both laughed again.

Fred got up to mop the floor, and Nick and Bob stared at him. "What about you?" Nick shouted. "You have a long way to go but still." The duo chuckled.

"Run a multi-billion-shilling company," Fred said flatly.

"While scrubbing the floor like that? I would say you're right on track," Nick shouted, and the duo laughed for what felt like a minute.

Fred left them to their laughter even though he still had an itch to ask Nick for his boss's contacts. He dried the floor, put the cleaning equipment back in the store, and headed for the TV room. While walking, he noticed that his nurse did not come to supervise his work nor escort him to the TV room.

He smiled as he sat down to watch *National Geographic*. A shark was swimming in the ocean and these tiny fish called remoras were eating the scraps on its body and, in doing so, feeding themselves and cleaning the shark at the same time. He would soon be a shark, he thought, and everyone else would be his remora fish.

The first thing he would do would be to fuel the jet or the yacht and fly or cruise around the world. Perhaps he would even get to see the sharks and the remoras in action. He had been trying to work towards a life of status and luxury when it was right under his nose. He laughed at the irony and started to doze off.

His nurse tapped him on the shoulder and woke him up for supper. Fred sat in the dining hall with a glass of water and a plate of rice, French beans, and fried liver. He had not taken a bite when Monica joined him with her tray of food.

"Sorry about last time. I was out of pocket," Fred apologized while biting a spoonful of food.

"It's okay. I was worse than you once," Monica said and sipped a glass of water.

Fred laughed.

"You don't believe me?"

"So what made you turn? Or as they say, what's your redemption story?" Fred asked after another spoonful of food.

Monica laughed. "How was your day?"

"Okay, actually. My headaches and nausea are receding."

"That's great news," she said while taking a spoonful from her plate. "Where do you spend your afternoons?" she asked after swallowing her food.

"In the TV room. Today I was watching this show about the shark and the remora fish," Fred began, and he didn't stop until his nurse tapped him on the shoulder to tell him it was time for bed.

He did not have a different shade of uniform waiting for him in his room, but for the first time in a long time, he felt that he could beat this. He felt he could make something of himself.

56.

Olivia

SHE WATCHED THE fan make its rounds and listened to the clinking of the crystals on the chandelier. She loved the fan now. It understood her. It did not reprimand her as her mother did. It did not hurt her like her boyfriend, Larry, nor pain her like Dr. Onyango. She watched it go round and round and round till it resembled a living thing.

"What's your name?" she asked.

The fan stared down at her and made its rounds.

"I'm Olivia, but my friends call me Liv. What about your friends?"

The fan made its rounds, wheezing like an asthmatic kid.

"Oh, you don't have any friends? Let me come and give you a hug."

Olivia got up from the couch and climbed the table. She could not reach it. She climbed up the stairs and leaned from the rails. She was now closer to it. She leaned further and further until she almost touched it, and she fell from the railing. She did not hear herself hit the ground. The world went dark before she did.

Gakenia was a big girl now; sharp and intelligent, just like her. She had just celebrated her 13th birthday, and she was asking those questions Olivia found uncomfortable.

"Where is Daddy? What is his name? What does he look like?"

Initially, Olivia had started by telling her that she did not have a father. When that did not work, she told her he had enrolled in the army and gotten killed in Somalia by *Al-Shabaab*. When that failed, Olivia resorted to the truth.

Larry had moved on to another woman, and they now lived happily in Donholm with two sons and a daughter. Even after hearing the story, Gakenia still wanted to know her dad. Olivia had called Larry, and they had arranged for him to meet her.

Gakenia dressed up excitedly, and within the hour, they were knocking on Larry's door, but no one was answering. They were almost giving up when the door creaked open. On the other side was Larry, armed with a smile.

"Come in. I was expecting you. How is my daughter doing?" he said in staccato—trying to overcompensate for all the years he had been absent from her life.

Olivia flashed a smile, and Gakenia beamed. She went to speak and ended up mumbling, her words caught in her throat.

"Come to the kitchen, Gakenia. I have made your favorite dish," Larry continued.

Olivia followed them to the kitchen, but there was no food. Larry turned around, but he was no longer Larry but Dr. Onyango. He got a sharp kitchen knife and started stabbing Gakenia: one time, two times, three times, countless times. Olivia woke up screaming. She was in her bed, nicely tucked in.

57.

Wairimu

HER OFFICE WAS small, with a milk-white desk and a red leather couch, but to her, it felt like a golf course. She sat down on her swiveling chair and stared at her spanking new MacBook Pro. She looked at it and felt grateful, even though she knew some suppliers somewhere might not have been paid on time for it to be purchased.

She stirred on her seat and glanced at the newspapers that Tatiana had placed at her desk. Tatiana had not spoken to her; she had placed them on her desk and left hurriedly. Wairimu picked the *Business Daily*. Reading felt better than ferrying, she realized, as one of the headlines jumped at her. "AJABU DIG-ITAL NO LONGER THE GIANT IT WAS," it read. Her jaw tightened, and she folded the newspapers in half before push-ing them aside.

She picked up her office phone and pretended to receive a call.

"Hello, Account Director of Mambo Tele maize flour speaking, how can I help you?"

"Hello, Wairimu here, Account Director Ajabu Digital speaking, how can I help you?"

"Hello, Wairimu speaking, how can I help you?"

She put the handset back on the receiver and swiveled on her chair. She looked at the plain walls and wondered if she should get a painting or a photo or two for them, but before she could decide, Chris entered her office.

"I heard the good news," he beamed.

"Who was the snitch? Was it Tatiana?" Wairimu said as they hugged.

"I told you, things get better when you look at the glass as half-full."

"I'm thankful."

"We should celebrate."

"I haven't even looked at my schedule. I will ring you," Wairimu said while looking at her phone.

"Ring me? Okay, Miss Account Director," Chris said with a high-pitched tone and dissolved out of her office.

Winfred and Kitana were the next ones in her office. They thought it a good gesture, but they did not know that by coming around her office, they were planting seeds for unnecessary rumors.

She had not caught a break when her phone rang. "Hello, Wairimu speaking, how can I help you?" she answered.

She was scheduled to have a mid-morning status meeting with her team. She picked her notebook and went to the boardroom to find Jackeline, Sam, and Ryan waiting for her.

Wairimu glanced at them—from the vibrant team she had met in the brainstorm, they now looked weary. They had not gotten past hello before her phone buzzed. She was scheduled to meet her clients at noon. She looked at her watch; it was 11:50 am. She rescheduled and excused herself.

In a few minutes, she was with Kitana in another boardroom, sitting down with two of Mambo Tele's advertising executives, discussing the year's strategy.

They handled them with grace and decorum, even though Mambo Tele owed them a few millions and were part of the reason Ajabu Digital was having cash flow problems.

The discussions went on till evening, and Wairimu found herself back at her desk, ordering takeout to eat while going through the brand's strategy. She took a break momentarily and looked at her notifications. She had three messages and five missed calls from Chris.

'Waiting for you at our restaurant.'

'Where are you?'

'Are you still coming?'

She decided she would respond to him later and unwrapped her Subway sandwich, took a swig from her Minute Maid juice, and continued going through the outdoor, TV, print, and social media strategy for Mambo Tele maize flour. She lifted her head at 5:00 pm and went to the washrooms.

She heard the whisper while getting ready to sit on the toilet bowl. "She's slept with Chris, Winfred, and Kitana—that's why she has moved from receptionist to Account Director in the blink of an eye," she heard a voice that resembled Tatiana's say.

"She's a whore. I have seen videos of her showing her breasts making rounds on the internet," someone whose voice she couldn't recognize was saying.

She got flashbacks of the *My Dress, My Choice* demo as the fingers of a headache started climbing up her spine. She put her hands on her temples as she heard more whispers about prison and terrible management until the voices receded and the washrooms went quiet.

Besides a headache, Wairimu now felt nauseated. She faced the toilet bowl and vomited her subway sandwich and Minute Maid juice. Her transition to Account Director had come complete with a welcome mat and a bowl of cookies with a bow on top.

58.

Unexpected Guest

It had been a little over three months since Fred checked into Meadows Rehabilitation Facility. His migraines and nausea had ebbed, and he was beginning to regain his weight and his youth. He got out of bed, had a shower, wore his blue uniform, and went to the dining room to have breakfast.

He sat with his tea, two slices of bread, and an omelet and watched new patients streaming in, manned by their nurses. He looked around for Monica, but he couldn't find her. She had been pumped up to a green uniform and had volunteered to be counseling the red and blue patients.

He ate his breakfast and realized he missed their conversations. Hopefully, he would find her in her arts and crafts class in the afternoon. She had convinced him to take up her class, and he had agreed. He now took the first part of her class before going to the TV room.

He finished his breakfast and walked to his first counseling session. Dr. Karani was seated with three new patients. Two were in red uniform, and the third one was in blue. Fred sat down and became the fourth.

"My name is Dr. Karani," he said after Fred took his seat. "We are going to go around while introducing ourselves and share our redemption stories." He passed the brown rod to an average-looking man with dark lips and dark fingers in blue uniform to his right. "After you are done sharing your story, pass the rod to the next person, and so on."

"My name is Moses," he started. "I am doing this for my own sanity. I am tired of waking up in terror at night, wondering which one among the people I owe money is coming to collect it," he said and passed the rod to a thin woman with broken teeth in a red uniform.

"I'm here because I was told I would get high…" she giggled. "Not to listen to boring stories," she added and began laughing in staccato while holding on to the brown rod.

Dr. Karani got up, took the rod from her, and passed it to a tall, slender woman who was also in a red uniform.

"My name is Irene. I'm here because I got high and hit my son while reversing my car, and he's now paralyzed in the ICU," she said, and tears welled in her eyes as she passed the rod to Fred. The woman with broken teeth had stopped laughing and was wearing a somber face.

"My name is Fred. I'm here because I want to make something out of myself besides getting high and masturbating in my room," Fred said before returning the rod to Dr. Karani.

***

FRED WALKED INTO his one-on-one session with Dr. Karani. They sat across from each other. Dr. Karani was very impressed with his progress. They talked about the beginning of his drug addiction—how he graduated from alcohol to weed to powder, and how he was using them as a substitute for the love and attention that was missing in his life.

Dr. Karani encouraged him to keep a notebook and write what he felt and why he felt it every time he thought of getting high. They shook hands, and he adjourned their session.

Fred walked to the dining hall for lunch. He looked around. He still couldn't find Monica. He ate his *matoke*, drank his glass of mango juice quickly, and went looking for her in her arts and crafts class.

Monica was leading the class in dancing steps.

"One, two, three, four. Then spin. Five, six, seven. Then bend. Eight, nine, and ten. Stand and spin." The class rehearsed the steps about five times before stopping for a 15-minute break.

"I figured that if I can't act, the least I can do is teach acting," Monica said to Fred.

"You're patient. That's a good quality for a teacher," Fred added.

"What do you plan to do when you get out of here?" she asked.

"I had a dream of becoming a musician, but I think I will just finish my finance degree."

"Come on, don't kill your dreams."

"There are more important things than dreams," Fred said, his voice trailing off. "What about you? What do you plan to do?"

"My place is here, teaching arts and crafts classes and counseling."

"Why?"

"I have seen enough of the world, and there's not much out there for me," Monica said as her students started streaming in for the second part of her acting class.

Fred excused himself. The first session had already exhausted him, and he did not want to miss his *National Geographic* show.

He walked to the TV room, wondering what could be going through someone's mind to make them leave all the world had to offer behind to stay in a grim place like this, to help a bunch of crackheads and lunatics recuperate. He sat down on his chair. He had not gotten his mind together when the intercom whirred, and his name was called. He had a visitor. He wondered who it could be when his mother had just visited recently.

59.

Helena

HELENA WAS SMOKING while seated on her queen bed in her Karen villa in a pink negligee that exposed her breasts and a lace thong. She placed her cigarette on the ashtray, held her hair into a ponytail and secured it with a pin before taking a long pull from her cigarette.

She was just from having a difficult phone call with her daughter, who had told her that she would be staying permanently at Meadows Rehabilitation Facility in Nanyuki to volunteer with the patients.

Such bad timing, she thought while blowing a cloud of smoke from her mouth and nostrils. She had just resigned from her TV-show-hosting job to focus on her daughter and on Helena Beauty Spa. She took another pull from her cigarette and let out a cloud of smoke.

She got out of bed, opened the door to her balcony, and felt the breeze massage her body. She scanned her backyard, looking for her shamba-boy, but he was nowhere to be found.

She had another pull from her cigarette while thinking about her previous job. If she hadn't resigned, she would have been fired. Many are the times she had not shown up to work, and rumors were already starting to spread about her sexual misconduct with junior employees.

She took another pull from her cigarette, let out a cloud of smoke, and went back to her queen bed. She stubbed out the cigarette on the ashtray, pulled her nightstand drawer open, and got the accounting books of Helena Beauty Spa. As she did, the Nairobi Revival Church pamphlet fell on the floor. She picked it up and stared at it before placing it on top of her nightstand and opening her company's books.

The figures gave her a headache. Her accountant had told her that they were nowhere close to being profitable. They were operating way beyond their means, and if her investor's funds were to fall off, Helena Beauty Spa would fall together with him.

Helena looked at the books again. She stared at the word investor and thought of Mzee Ajabu. "He will always be there for me," she said to herself.

She turned the page and read her accountant's notes. Besides bringing to an end the extension of free services to her friends, he suggested they cut back the number of employees by half, eliminate some of the luxurious offerings in the business like steam rooms and saunas, and move to a modest location. That way, they could be profitable within a year and start thinking of expansion.

Helena looked at the suggestions and creased her forehead. How could she cut back now when everybody was expecting her to fail—especially now that she had quit her job? "He will always be there for me," she said to herself again and decided that she would ask for another three million Kenya shillings to expand the business. She smiled at the thought and reached for her packet of Embassy Lights.

She lit another cigarette and took a long pull before getting out of bed again and going to her balcony. She scanned the backyard for her shamba-boy, but he was still nowhere to be found.

She went to the front door and scanned the front lawn. It was empty except for her Mercedes S350, which stood sentry in the parking lot. "Fuck," she cursed, then laughed after remembering that she had given him the day off. *He works so hard,* she thought. She took another pull from her cigarette and blew a cloud of smoke while climbing the stairs and pushing the door to her master bedroom open.

She sat on her queen bed, stubbed out her cigarette on the ashtray, and pulled open her drawer. She came out with a large vibrator designed in the shape of a big, black penis. She turned it on, and it shook her hands as it vibrated. Her pupils dilated in excitement.

She pushed aside her lace thong and pushed it inside her. "He will always be there for me," she gasped before turning her thoughts to her shamba-boy, and her master bedroom was filled with vibration sounds and groans.

60.

Jack

JACK DID NOT realize he had hit the jackpot with Fred until later on. Like most of his weed clients, he thought he was another average guy on campus looking to have a bit of fun with his pocket money before he grew out of the habit.

Even when he gave him the free bag of powder, he was unsure. He was just throwing mud on the wall to see if it would stick. He had thought it had been a loss until Fred called him, and even when he did, he thought it would be the beginning of Fred's decline, but he never thought it would be the start of his ascent.

Powder was expensive. He was sure Fred would spend the little money he had, and maybe sell his possessions before he went bust. It was not until Fred gave him the location of where he stayed, and Jack saw their house while delivering him the batch, that he thought maybe he was on to something with Fred.

After that, the relationship between them started looking

up. He brought him three original luxury brand watches worth a quarter of a million, and Jack realized that perhaps he had found a cash cow.

Things only got better after that. Fred broke into his father's safe and brought Jack the half a million Kenya shillings that was in it. It was then that Jack's interest was piqued, and he sent Jamuel to survey him.

Jamuel had come with nothing but good news. Fred's father was Mzee Ajabu, the founder and CEO of Ajabu Digital, and Fred was his heir. That was when Jack knew he had hit the jackpot.

There was only one problem. Fred was in a rehab facility in Nanyuki, on his way to recovery. That was bad for his business, Jack realized, and that was how he found himself fabricating documents that said he was Fred's personal doctor. And that was how he got into Jamuel's Porsche Cayenne and found himself at Meadows Rehabilitation Facility, telling the management that he wanted to review his patient's progress.

61.

Relapse

THEY SAT IN the field. Jack was in a black suit, white shirt, and a red tie, with glasses on the bridge of his nose. He had even removed the gold coating on his tooth, and he almost resembled Dr. Karani.

"How did you get in here?" Fred asked with a raised brow.

Jack put his glasses on his forehead and looked at Fred properly. He smelled of soap, and he no longer looked anxious like he used to. This would be harder than he had thought it would be, he was realizing.

"I am a man of means, but if you must know, I am here in the capacity of your personal doctor." Jack removed a Nairobi Hospital doctor's tag from the inside of his coat and flashed it at Fred.

"What are you doing here?" Fred asked.

"I should be asking you that question. What the fuck are you doing here, Freddie boy?"

"Getting better from all the shit you sold me," Fred said while getting up.

"Shit? I sold you clean stuff. It took you to places you've never been before, didn't it?" Jack said, also getting up and opening the button on his coat to reveal his red tie.

Fred's eyes flashed for a split second as he remembered the high. "I am no longer that person. Why are you here?" he asked again.

"To save you from this fucked up place."

"Fucked up? This is the place that is going to make me the man."

"How?"

"Family stuff, you wouldn't understand."

"Come on, Freddie boy, you think I'm stupid? You think I don't know you're Mzee Ajabu's son?" He paused. "Tell me, do you think your dad is stupid enough to hand his company to a crackhead?"

Fred's eyes glazed over. "He doesn't know."

"Monica, the girl you flirt around with here, is your bastard sister, and she is not in your father's last will and testament." Fred was now rooted to the spot, open-mouthed. "I told you I'm a man of means. I know everything."

"I…I need to speak to my mom first," Fred stammered.

"Your sister, Wairimu, is already set up in Ajabu Digital to replace your dad. She started working there about six months ago. Or is it a year? I'm not sure." Jack paused. "There is no way your dad is handing a crackhead his life's work. Not a chance in hell," he said and started laughing.

"Wairimu…is…an activist," Fred stammered some more.

"No, she's intelligent. She's taken your birthright from right under your nose like you're some sucker—well, your dad wasn't going to give it to you in the first place, so you decide who is worse."

Fred's face contorted, and he stared into space. "I...I...I need to speak to my mom first."

"What you need to do is to think straight," Jack said while getting into his coat pocket and coming out with a bag of powder. He poured some of it into a line on his hand. "Forget what they have been telling you. Here is your freedom and your chance to be the man."

Fred hesitated for a split second, then closed his left nostril, leaned into Jack, and snorted the powder.

"What should we do now?" he asked.

"We take everything from everyone who has wronged you as a lesson for messing with you."

They walked into the facility's reception area, and Jack started raising hell about their sedation and detoxifying drugs and how they were having side effects on his client. After a few minutes, Fred was in the back-left seat of Jamuel's Porsche Cayenne—Jack in the passenger seat and Jamuel in the driver's seat, driving at 120kilometers per hour—headed towards his Runda home.

62.

Wairimu

THE GOSSIP GOING around spiraled out of control after Wairimu started spending huge amounts of time in Kitana's office. Some employees thought the worst of her even though Kitana was just taking her through the budgets and profit projections—looking for areas that could save the company money.

"Thank you for a job well done with Mambo Tele maize flour," Kitana had told her. Mambo Tele maize flour had been a contractual client for the longest time, but after Wairimu got into the picture, it had cleared its debt and become a retainer client.

"Don't mention it; it was the least I could do," she had said, the citrus in Kitana's Paco Rabanne staining her nose. Kitana took her hand and placed it on their biggest miscellaneous expense as the jasmine in her Black Opium stained his.

He was having a hard time admitting to himself that he had taken a liking to her—she was a natural leader, and she had a gift for executing difficult tasks effortlessly.

"That's your father's petty cash. It runs Ajabu Digital anywhere from eight to ten million Kenya shillings every month," Kitana had said.

"What?" Wairimu had gasped in shock. "That's enough money to cover a month's salary for the entire creative department!"

"Tell me about it."

"Where does the money go?"

"Where do I start? Let's see. There is the helicopter, the private jet, and his yacht, but even that is still not enough to run us eight to ten million a month in the hole."

"So where is the money going?"

"Only your father can tell you that."

"You and I both know he won't."

They had looked at each other and smiled.

"The helicopter, jet, and yacht—are they needed?"

"The helicopter is handy with quick movements around the country. The jet helps with executive meetings around the world, but the yacht is debatable. It swallows up a lot of money in maintenance costs and dock fees alone."

"Let me guess. It's not going to go up for sale any time soon?" Wairimu had asked, and they had paused, looked at each other, and smiled again.

"By the way, I want you to start attending finance and operation meetings," Kitana had said casually.

"What about Mambo Tele maize flour?"

"Delegate parts of the job to Ryan. If we're going to save this company, I'm going to need you by my side."

They smiled some more before getting back to reviewing Ajabu Digital's books of accounting.

***

WAIRIMU'S FREE TIME had thinned. She got to work early in the morning and left late at night. She did not have time to take lunch breaks with Chris. Raincheck after raincheck, and Chris had gotten tired, and it was in that way that he got involved in the office gossip.

"Kitana, of all people. Isn't he 40? What is he doing with a campus girl?" he had whispered sourly to Tatiana when she dropped his newspapers.

Even though gossip about her was everywhere, her work spoke for itself. Her team had also stepped up to the plate in the short time she had led them, and they handled Mambo Tele maize flour remarkably with very little help from her.

She had done it by opening communication lines and making sure that team members could ask for help from each other so that there was no one time that any of them was overwhelmed.

There was an excitement for work in her team that had never been there before. The team often joked that she had made work fun.

The budgets and profit projections weren't fun, though. Every evening, Wairimu closed the heavy profit-and-loss files that sat in front of her and breathed a sigh, only to open them again when she got home.

They had hired an auditing firm to help them put a solid case together so they could start approaching banks. Kitana had told her that such deals were made over golf and whiskey, but she had convinced herself that she would do it by the book, that she would put up such a strong argument that any bank would be crazy not to take up the opportunity.

It had become a routine of hers. After she was done for the day, she would walk into her father's office and gaze at the chair and at the scenic view of Nairobi at night. She would touch the leather seat and imagine herself as the CEO of Ajabu Digital.

63.

Mzee Ajabu

MZEE AJABU WALKED into his house, frustrated. He was just from another golfing game with another banker who did not fold. "I will get back to you my ass," he cursed. "Maybe I should visit Helena and blow off some steam," he said to himself while plopping onto the sofa.

He had not sat for long when he saw someone going to the kitchen. He picked up a broom and followed them. He dropped the broom, shocked upon realizing it was Olivia. She was a shadow of the person he used to know: her hair was shaved, and her frame was stick-thin.

"Olivia," he whispered. "Is that you?" he asked.

Olivia was deep in a daydream. Her daughter, Gakenia, was in the Intensive Care Unit, full of stab wounds, and she needed blood badly. She picked up a kitchen knife and placed the sharp end on her wrist while muttering.

"It will be okay, Gakenia; mommy is here."

"It will be okay, Gakenia; mommy is here."

"It will be okay, Gakenia; mommy is here."

Mzee Ajabu stood rooted at the door, dazed by what was happening. It was only after Olivia slit her wrist and blood started dripping on the floor that he got out of his stupor and ran towards her.

"What are you doing?" he barked while taking the knife from her hands and wrapping a cloth around the wound.

He reached for his phone and dialed their family doctor. The number was busy.

He picked up Olivia and carried her to his Range Rover. The gate was wide open, with a Porsche Cayenne blocking the entry.

Whose car is that, and where are the guard and my driver? Mzee Ajabu wondered while buckling his daughter's seat belt.

Olivia was still muttering.

"It will be okay, Gakenia; mommy is here."

"It will be okay, Gakenia; mommy is here."

"It will be okay, Gakenia; mommy is here."

64.

Homecoming

FRED JUMPED OUT of the Porsche Cayenne, wearing a mask and holding a gun: a Glock 19 that he had been given by Jack. His head lolled twice; it felt loose on his shoulders.

"Get out of the car, old man," he barked at his father as he finished buckling in his sister.

"Fred, is that you?" Mzee Ajabu asked, dazed, as Jack disappeared into their house and Jamuel finished tying up the driver and the guard.

"You don't want trouble, old man. Give us the keys to your car, and we will be out of your hair."

"Your sister is dying. At least let us take her to hospital," Mzee Ajabu pleaded.

"I don't give a shit about her. She can go to hell for all I care," Fred barked, thinking it was Wairimu. "Get her out of the car and leave her on the grass," he said to no one in particular.

Jamuel tucked his gun into his waistband, unbuckled Olivia

from her seat, and threw her onto the grass like a sack of potatoes.

Fred went through his father's pockets and came out with the car keys. He then knocked his forehead with the butt of his Glock, and Mzee Ajabu fell on the grass, bleeding.

"Fred, what has gotten into you?" he whimpered.

"Shut up, old man," Jamuel knocked his forehead again with the heel of his boot before disappearing into the house.

After a few minutes, the two men came out of Mzee Ajabu's house with every piece of jewelry and all the money they could find.

They removed their masks. Jack got into the Range Rover with Fred, and Jamuel got into the Porsche Cayenne.

Mzee Ajabu watched his son drive off in disbelief, then looked at his daughter hemorrhaging on the grass, and he started convulsing, slowly at first, then erratically. The stroke finally hit him like a bag of bricks falling from the sky.

65.

Wairimu

Wairimu's taxi got to their gate, and she unbuckled her seatbelt. She glanced at the Ajabu Digital accounting files sitting on her lap for what felt like a minute—she had been carrying work home for a while now. She had even forgotten about her family. She wondered what her mom, brother, and sister were up to before putting the files in her bag and opening the car door.

"Madam," she heard the taxi driver call her.

She smiled, embarrassed, getting into her bag to pay the fare.

She was thinking of buying her own car. Kitana had suggested a Volkswagen Golf for her first car.

"You can't go wrong with a German machine," he had said.

He drove a Volkswagen Tuareg himself. She thought of him and smiled while getting out of the car and closing the door.

She watched the taxi reverse, then she turned and started walking towards their house. Their gate was open, and their guard was nowhere to be seen. "That's strange," she mumbled while closing it.

She called his name while scanning the compound. It did not take long before she saw the two bodies looking lifeless on the grass. She rushed towards them, then stood frazzled for an entire minute when she realized it was her dad and small sister.

"Olivia! Olivia! What happened? What happened?" she pleaded, panicked.

Olivia was still convulsing. The open wound where she had cut herself was still oozing blood. Her dad looked pale. He had an open wound on his forehead, and his eyes had rolled up.

Wairimu looked at Oliva, and tears pricked her eyes and rolled down her cheeks as she got on her knees to inspect her pulse. It was beating softly. She knew she had to move quickly if she was going to save her.

She removed her phone from her bag, but it slipped and fell. She picked it up to dial Dr. Onyango, and it beeped with a 'battery low' notification and switched off. She got out of the gate and stopped a *boda-boda*.

The rider helped her with Olivia. Wairimu hesitated for a second before they went back for her dad, and within a few minutes, they were both sandwiched between her and the rider, speeding towards Nairobi Hospital.

66.

Mrs. Ajabu

Mrs. Ajabu came back from buying groceries for supper. The first thing she did after their guard gave her the news was place the groceries on the kitchen counter, open her small fridge, and get a fresh bottle of wine. She reached for her large wine glass, before placing it back on the shelf and taking a swig from the bottle.

"It can't be my son, Fred. I just saw him a few days ago. It can't be him," she muttered under her breath and took a long swig from the bottle of wine. *I saw him a few days ago. He was getting better. It can't be my Fred. He's a good boy. He wouldn't do anything like that,* she thought and took another long swig.

"It must be peer pressure," she muttered under her breath again.

The wine and the truth made her dizzy, and she staggered and knocked the groceries from the kitchen counter: Oranges, beetroot, tomatoes, and onions scattered all over the floor.

Something else had also fallen. Rat poison. She picked it up quickly, put it in her pocket, and staggered into the sitting room with her bottle of wine.

The fan was doing its rounds, and the crystals on the chandelier clinked. Mrs. Ajabu pulled off her wig, threw it on the floor, and started pulling her *matuta*. "No, no, no, no!" she shouted. "This is not how things were supposed to go," she said while taking another gulp of wine.

How reckless is the rehabilitation facility? another thought crossed her mind. *I should have words with them and make them understand who they're dealing with.* She took another swig from her bottle after realizing how little reprimanding the rehabilitation facility would accomplish.

She placed the bottle on the table, got into her pocket, and came out with the rat poison. She stared at it, thought of her husband, and started laughing loudly. She took another swig from her bottle as her laughing turned into sobbing.

She wiped her tears with the back of her hand, then stared at the ceiling and watched the fan make its rounds and listened to the clinking of the chandelier. "Am I becoming my daughter?" she grumbled. "I saved her. I saved her from shame and embarrassment. She will thank me someday. She will thank me," her tone was rising. "I know she will."

Who will take over the company now? she wondered. "No, no, no. Not Wairimu," she said. "It's all going wrong." She pulled her *matuta* and took another swig from her bottle. She stared at the ceiling again. The fan became hazy, and the clinking of the chandelier started fading.

"Where is Fred? Should I call the police?" she muttered and lifted the bottle to her lips, but it was empty. "Fuck," she cursed as the empty bottle fell from her hand and rolled underneath the table.

"Where is Fred? Should I call the police?" she muttered again as her world started spinning and then went dark.

67.

Family Reunion

WAIRIMU WAS IN the private wing of Nairobi Hospital, next to her dad. His head was bandaged, and IV tubes ran through his body as his chest moved up and down with the help of a ventilator. She stared at him for a while before averting her gaze to the headline of the newspaper she was holding.

"MZEE AJABU HOSPITALIZED IN CRITICAL CONDITION," a small section of the newspaper read. She folded it in half, placed it next to her dad, and moved her gaze to her mom.

Her mom looked hungover in her long, baggy dress, headgear, and dark sunglasses. She was seated next to Mzee Ajabu, staring out the window. "Mom, are you okay?" Wairimu asked amidst the beeping of the cardiac monitor.

"Mom? Mom?"

"What?" Mrs. Ajabu stirred, irritated, as if she had been deep in a dream.

"Are you okay?"

"I'm fine."

"Should I get you some tea?"

"I'm fine."

Wairimu moved her gaze back to her dad and wondered how much time he had left. She had not completed the thought when a nurse knocked on the door and entered, pushing Olivia on a wheelchair.

Olivia had recuperated from her knife wound, but she did not remember herself. The doctors had diagnosed her with a severe case of retrograde amnesia. Her papers for Meadows Rehabilitation Facility were being processed. Wairimu had settled the bill for the facility in full with the money she had saved up to buy a car.

"Where am I? Who are these people?" Olivia asked.

Wairimu looked at her sister and thought of her brother, and her jaw tightened. *I will kill him,* she thought, kneeling in front of Olivia. A lone tear rolled down her cheek and left a dark patch on the carpet. "You're in hospital, Liv. That's Mom, and that's Dad," she said while wiping the tear with the back of her hand.

Wairimu blinked, and more tears rolled down her cheeks. She got up and wiped them with the hem of her blouse and glanced at her dad. The cardiac monitor beeped while his chest moved up and down to the whirring of the ventilator. She moved her gaze to her mother. She was still staring out the window behind her dark sunglasses.

"Mom? Mom?" she called again.

"What?" Mrs. Ajabu barked.

"Are you okay?"

"I'm fine."

"You know..." Wairimu paused, trying to get the words.

"Meadows could help you with your problem."

"I don't have a problem," Mrs. Ajabu barked again.

"Just say the word, and I will handle it."

"I'm fine. Everything will be okay soon. You will see," Mrs. Ajabu said and got back to staring out the window.

Before Wairimu could construct another sentence, the door flew open. Behind it was a stranger with a ragged face and in tattered clothes. A nurse was running behind him, shouting, "You can't go in there! You can't go in there!"

"Shut up. Do you know who I am? My dad could get you fired just like that."

It was only after he spoke that Wairimu recognized the voice was her brother's. Her jaw tightened again.

"What are you doing here? Get out," Wairimu barked.

"Who are these people?" Olivia asked softly.

"Who do you think you are to tell me to get out?" Fred responded.

"Get out. Mom, tell him to get out."

Mrs. Ajabu stayed silent and continued staring out the window—the slightest hint of a smile had touched her face.

"I'm not going anywhere; he's my dad too," Fred barked as a nurse walked in with guards, and they were escorted out.

Immediately they got to the corridor, Fred started sobbing.

"It was peer pressure, Mom. Forgive me."

"Who are these people?" Olivia said softly.

"I have nowhere to go. I'm broke," Fred sobbed.

"If he stays, I will leave," Wairimu said, defeated.

68.

Helena

HELENA AND HER muscled shamba-boy were sprawled naked in her queen bed in her Karen villa. Helena was tracing a long nail along the vein of his bicep. "Does it hurt?" she groaned, and her shamba-boy shook his head sideways. She went to trace the vein again but was stopped by the ringing of her phone.

She picked it up and replied with mmh's and uh's. Her face sagged, and she looked pale after she thumbed the red receiver button.

"Madam kila kitu iko sawa?" her shamba-boy asked. She saw his mouth moving, but she did not hear the words it was saying.

She got out of bed, wore a lime-green gown, picked up her pack of Embassy Lights, and went to the balcony. She let the breeze massage her body for a while before tapping out a cigarette and lighting it.

She took a long pull and blew a cloud of smoke from her mouth and nostrils. She had just received a call from Tatiana informing her that Mzee Ajabu had suffered a stroke, and he was in critical condition at the Intensive Care Unit in Nairobi Hospital.

She took another pull from her cigarette. *No wonder he didn't reply to my text about the extra three million shillings,* she thought while blowing a cloud of smoke into the sky. She would need to down-size her business for sure. Her forehead creased as the thought crossed her mind.

She looked around her villa and took another pull from her cigarette. She would also need to move to a more modest house. Preferably an apartment in a middle-class location. The thought made her stomach churn.

She made to take another pull from her cigarette, but only the butt was left. She crushed it on the balcony railing and threw it into the wastebasket.

She tapped another cigarette out of the packet, lit it, and took a long pull. Her accountant would probably advise her to downgrade her Mercedes to something like a Nissan or a Toyota, she thought while blowing another cloud of smoke into the sky, and her stomach clenched further.

"He will make it," she said to herself, taking long pulls from her cigarette and blowing clouds of smoke into the sky.

She crushed the second butt on the railing of the balcony, threw it into the wastebasket, and tapped out another stick. She got back to her master bedroom and crushed the half-smoked cigarette on her ashtray. She stared at the Nairobi Revival Church pamphlet on top of her nightstand for a while before removing her gown and getting back to bed.

"Madam, kila kitu iko sawa?" her shamba-boy asked again.

"Kila kitu iko sawa," she said. She did not have the courage to tell him that he might be losing his job soon. Instead, she got on top of him and felt him stiffen inside of her. "He will make

it," she gasped as she dug her fingernails into her shamba-boy's chest and her queen bed began to squeak.

69.

Diana

While Mzee Ajabu was breathing through a ventilator, Diana was at the tennis court.

"Start with the racket in front of you and shift your weight to your right foot," her middle-aged trainer was saying. "And then serve," he added.

Diana tried to do as she was told and hit the ball out of the court.

"Let's try that again," her trainer was saying, but she wasn't hearing him. "Diana, are you listening?"

"Give me a second," she said while walking to her training bag and removing her iPhone. She dialed Mzee Ajabu again. He did not pick up. She thumbed the green receiver button again and put her phone on her ear. "Please pick up, please pick up," she murmured. "Shit," she cursed when the line went dead again.

He must be in a meeting, she convinced herself while walking back to her trainer. She handed him her phone and asked him to take photos of her. She was in a pink cap, black tank top, pink shorts, and pink Nike shoes. She posed this way and that, and the trainer took photos while admiring her.

She scrolled through the photos and selected the best one. *Serving legs today. #OOTD #StayFit,* she captioned the photo, posted it on her Instagram profile, and got back to her tennis training.

"Start with the racket in front of you and shift your weight to your right foot and serve," the trainer repeated his instructions, but Diana wasn't listening.

"Diana! Diana!" he shouted.

"I'm sorry, I'm just distracted," she apologized.

"Let's pause for today. We will pick it up again next week," he said and left the court.

Diana walked to the changing room and called Mzee Ajabu again. "Please pick up, please pick up," she murmured. "Shit," she cursed when the line went dead. *Is he ignoring me?* she wondered while pacing the length of the changing room. *No, no, no. I do too much for him to ignore me,* she thought, biting her nails.

She had a shower and changed into a denim jacket, Versace miniskirt, and flip-flops. She took a mirror selfie. *Never had to show off, only had to show up,* she captioned it and posted it on her Instagram profile.

She got into her BMW and drove to her Lavington apartment. Her house-help had made *chapatis*. She took a photo of them. *Home is where chapos are,* she captioned the photo and shared it on her Instagram stories.

She picked up a *chapo* and bit into it, but she could not stomach it. She put it back in the hotpot and went to her balcony to see if she could get a hold of Mzee Ajabu. His line was not going through. "Shit," she cursed and left the balcony.

She sat on the couch and switched the TV to *E!* to watch

Keeping up with the Kardashians. She looked at the screen without watching the show, wondering if Mzee Ajabu had blocked her.

Has he replaced me? The thought crossed her mind more than once. *He can't replace me, not after all I do for him,* she decided as beads of sweat formed on her nose and forehead.

70.

Moving Out

Mzee Ajabu's helicopter landed at Meadows Rehabilitation Facility, and Wairimu got out and helped Olivia down the steps of the chopper. Behind her were Kitana and their family doctor.

"For once, this helicopter is being used for good," Kitana thought without knowing that he was saying the words out loud.

"I know. I just wish the good wasn't bringing my sister to a rehab center," Wairimu responded.

Dr. Onyango disappeared to the administration block as Kitana, Wairimu, and Olivia walked to the hostel block. Kitana remained outside as Wairimu and her sister entered the hostel.

"Who are you?" Olivia asked softly as Wairimu was helping her put on her red uniform.

Wairimu's eyes became glassy again. She wiped her eyes with the back of her hand and knelt in front of her.

"I'm your sister, Wairimu. You are in Meadows Rehabilitation Facility. You will be admitted here for a while so you can get better.”

“What’s wrong with me?”

“There’s nothing wrong with you. You’re just sick, but you will get better.”

“Who are you?” Olivia asked again.

Wairimu stood up and wiped her eyes with the back of her hand again.

“Hello, my name is Monica. I will take it from here,” the nurse that was assigned to her was saying.

“Thank you,” Wairimu said and looked at her sister one more time before she turned the door handle and went looking for Kitana. She found him talking to Dr. Onyango.

“They will put her on psychotherapy and hypnosis treatment to help her regain her memory,” he said when Wairimu joined them.

“How long will it take for her to get back to normal?” Wairimu asked.

“With amnesia, it’s hard to tell. Sometimes the treatment is immediate, other times it takes years.”

“Is there a way I can help?” Warimu asked as they got into the chopper’s cabin.

“At this point, it’s all up to her to fight,” Dr. Onyango said with finality as the blades of the helicopter came alive, and they lifted off from Meadows Rehabilitation Facility in Nanyuki and headed for Nairobi.

***

WAIRIMU WAS MOVING out of their Runda mansion to a two-bedroom apartment in Pangani. She packed her books then stopped momentarily to look for her teddy bear. It was nowhere to be seen. She picked up Chinua Achebe’s *No Longer at Ease* and stared at it for a while and smiled. It was a book that started so many wars in her, she remembered.

She put it back in the box and glanced at the *My Dress, My Choice* placards that were leaning on the wall, and memories flooded her. She remembered the rotten tomatoes, the teargas, and the prison cell and smiled again.

"That's the last of the boxes," she heard Kitana shout at someone as she picked the box with her books.

She stared at her now empty room and felt nostalgic—she had grown from a little girl to a woman here, she thought, and now she was finding it hard to say goodbye. "If only rooms could be packed and carried," she mumbled, and her jaw tightened.

She closed the door behind her and started walking down the stairs to the living room. As she did, she heard chatter about off-peak hospital hours and disabling CCTV cameras. She got to their living room and found her mother, brother, their family doctor, and two other men she did not recognize. They went silent immediately they saw her.

She glanced at them and wondered what they were planning. One of the men she could not recognize was playing with her teddy bear. She smiled before opening the door and joining Kitana. The moving lorry was loaded and ready to take her to her new home.

71.

Wairimu

Wairimu was called to the boardroom immediately after she got into her office. She walked in to find the company executives there: Kitana, the Chief Financial Officer, Chief Information Officer, Chief Creative Officer, and the Chief Human Resource Officer. They were going to put to a vote for Kitana to be appointed as the interim Chief Executive Officer.

Wairimu did not know it by then, but her vote had the biggest weight. She was the only one in the room with a board seat. The vote was unanimous, with 100% of the room voting for Kitana as the interim CEO.

Kitana was flushed, as if he had not expected it, but in essence, he was the favorite. If Ajabu Digital stood, it was because of his superior management skills. Even though they were thwarted often by Mzee Ajabu and the cutthroat culture he had cultivated.

"Thank you," he said after clearing his throat. "I want to

start by offering my condolences to Wairimu for what happened to her father. We all love him here, and we wish him a quick recovery."

Wairimu nodded, and Kitana continued.

"The job of CEO is not easy. God knows that of COO was hard enough, but the same God has given us a wonderful team that should see daily tasks done while we try and sort out our cash flow problems." He paused. "My first order of business is to appoint an interim COO, someone I can work alongside," he continued. "Someone who shares the same beliefs that going forward will see us better placed in the industry."

The Assistant COO fidgeted in her chair. This had been the moment she had been waiting for. Kitana could not remember how she had become his assistant because she appeared to be the type of person who threw everyone she came across under the bus, and their bodies had piled up so high that she had used them as a ladder on her way to the top.

"You have all seen her around. She started by ferrying newspapers and as a receptionist, and she did it in the most meticulous and humble way. She has been nothing but a superstar account director, even with the false rumors going around about her. And even though the rumors might get worse, I'm going to make her interim COO because deep down, I know she is the antidote this company has been waiting for. Wairimu, can you stand?"

Wairimu was surprised by the news. *If you had told me, I could have dressed better,* she thought in her black trouser suit, red blouse, and black high heels as she stood up.

"This was completely unexpected. I'm at a loss for words." She paused and cleared her voice. "I've been going through the company books with Mr. Kitana, and let me just say, I have my work cut out for me. I guess from today I won't know what daylight looks like, eh boss?"

Everybody laughed except for the Assistant COO.

"I'm looking forward to working with you in the coming days, Mr. Kitana," she continued. "Our biggest task is to get Ajabu Digital out of the red in matters cash flow, but this should not trouble other departments. Continue executing your duties as you have, and let this be our monkey to worry about," she said finally and took her seat as the room applauded.

Wairimu walked to the office kitchenette to make a cup of coffee after the meeting.

"She destroyed her family so she could take over the company," she heard stifled whispers.

She pushed open the door to find Tatiana and the tea lady. She said hello to them, made her coffee, and went to Kitana's office. *My new office now,* she thought while sitting down. She started moving the papers on her desk. There was one that stared at her. She took it and looked at it keenly. It was a resignation letter from the Assistant COO.

Family Feuds

The fault, dear Brutus, is not in our stars, but in ourselves.

- William Shakespeare, *Julius Caesar*

72.

Wairimu

THE DAYS HAD faded quickly. Wairimu looked at the calendar on the wall, and she couldn't believe that over six months had passed since her tenure as COO began. She glanced at the newspaper on her desk. "AJABU DIGITAL RECLAIMS ITS POSITION IN THE INDUSTRY," it read, with a full-size photo of her standing next to Kitana.

She closed it and folded it in half. She still couldn't believe that their cash flows were becoming positive. Well, most of their profits were going into paying their debts, but that would only be for a time.

At first, Wairimu and Kitana seemed to have run out of ideas. Every bank was turning them down. Until it finally hit Wairimu. She could sell her 25% stake of the company to the public. That way, they would have enough money to run the company, and it would still be family-owned, with her dad, brother, and sister having the majority of the shares.

Together with Kitana, she had started by vetting the stakeholders. They did not want iron-clad shareholders. They wanted people who shared their vision.

They divided the shares into class A and B. Wairimu and Kitana took a 5% stake each of class A shares, and they divided another 10% to heavy hitters and the other 5% to the public.

After the offering, Tom, the CEO of Kenya International Bank, approached them, placing on the table the same offer he had refused Mzee Ajabu—to be the company's bank of choice, with a package of 800 million initial equity and monthly operational costs. But there were other offers as well.

Wairimu found herself going with the leaner offer of 400 million shillings a month from Commercial Bank of Africa, believing in her gut that a time would come when cash flow would not be an issue. She had set this in motion by opening a contingent account for the company. She looked at the account on her MacBook. It now had 100 million Kenya shillings and was growing. She had made up her mind that 30% of the contingent account would go towards employees' bonuses at the end of the year.

Employees were another thorny issue. She had sat down with Kitana and combed through them. Even though the majority had toxic tendencies, they agreed that that was not who they were at their core, and they decided to give them a chance. They did this by opening a training wing in the topmost floor of their offices. The HR department went through their core values and what needed to be done to achieve their long-term goals. Departments would no longer be departments but teams, with a team leader.

They started by giving a grace period of three months. Those who didn't follow through were given warning letters and, after that, dismissal letters. Tatiana and Chris were the first ones to be dismissed.

Wairimu's jaw had tightened when she got the news of Chris's dismissal, remembering her friendship with him when she first joined. But then it had relaxed as she decided that she needed to make the hard decisions if they were going to grow. After that, the turnover had reduced to less than 1%.

***

Wairimu steadied herself in her office chair. She looked in every way a CEO—settled and well-adjusted. She removed the earphones from her ears, closed the record player on her phone, and tapped on the browser. She cleared her history on car rentals, Nairobi Hospital scrubs, and ventilators.

She glanced at her Burberry watch. It read 10:00 am. She had an investors' meeting set for 10:15 am. She picked up her iPad and Apple pencil and headed to the boardroom. All the stakeholders with class A shares were present, with the exception of Olivia, Mzee Ajabu, and Fred.

Wairimu began by taking them through operations—where the company was and where it was headed. The CFO took over after she was done and went through the numbers, followed by the CHRO, who went through the new wing. "We have rebranded the new wing to Talent and Training. Employees will now work in posts according to their strength," she finished, and Kitana got up.

"It is good to see the company going in the right direction. When Mzee Ajabu gets well, he will be proud," he said and cleared his voice. "This was a dream of ours, and now the dream has become a reality." The room was rapturous in applause.

"I do not deserve an ounce of that praise. It should all go to Wairimu."

Wairimu nodded her head and mouthed, "It was a team

effort."

Kitana smiled. "As you all know, I have been interim CEO for some time now, and I feel it's time for someone deserving to fill those shoes. Wairimu has gotten to a place where she is more than capable of filling those shoes, and I can go back to my COO position. I'm not sure what I will be doing exactly, since she has been managing everything meticulously. Maybe I will make her coffee, eh Wairimu? Will you give me that honor?"

Wairimu chuckled, wondering what he was saying when the whole company knew they would be lost without him. Mzee Ajabu had gotten to a place where he had become more esthetics than management, and it was Kitana who took up his job.

"If there are no objections, I would like the board members who are here to sign the papers that are sitting in front of you, confirming Wairimu as Chief Executive Officer of Ajabu Digital as of today."

They had not had a second glance at the papers when the door flew open. Behind it was Mzee Ajabu's lawyer, Fred, and Mrs. Ajabu.

73.

Hostile Takeover

"WHERE ARE YOUR MANNERS? You mean you can have such an important meeting without all the stakeholders?" Fred started. He had cleaned up well, in a custom-made black suit and golden Rolex watch. He looked in every way like a younger version of Mzee Ajabu.

"Last I checked, we own this company. Oh wait, my dear sister over here sold her birthright for a bowl of soup. Yet, here she is, being anointed. Where is the wisdom in that?" he continued.

"If you looked at our books keenly, you would have noticed that we had a cash flow problem. But I imagine, if it doesn't get you high, your crack head finds it difficult to understand," Wairimu barked, her kettle of composure coming to a boil and its lid falling off.

"My crack head understands a lot of things that you, with all your business acumen, don't. For example, it understands that

I am next in line after Dad. It's time to hand over the keys to the Lamborghini. Your test drive is over."

"I believe that's not your decision to make but the stakeholders'. I still have majority shareholding, with Dad and Olivia on my side."

"Do you, dear sister?" Fred asked. "Our small sister, may God give her a quick recovery, is a lunatic. And our dad, well, God rest his soul, is no more. You know what, I will let his lawyer take over from here," he said with finality.

Mrs. Ajabu was silent the entire time, even though she was the orchestrator of all this. A part of her was remorseful, another excited that she was about to get all she ever wanted.

"In the event of my death, my estate shall be divided equally among my children," The lawyer began reading Mzee Ajabu's last will and testament. "My company structure shall be as follows," he continued. "Olivia Ajabu shall serve as CHRO, Wairimu Ajabu as the COO under the condition that she passes her training, and my son, Fred Ajabu, shall serve as CEO," he said finally.

"Who is to even say you have passed your training?" Fred laughed. "Ladies and gentlemen, I think it is only fair that you tear the papers in front of you, and say hello to your new CEO," he said finally with a big smile across his face.

74.

Final Journey

It had been a quiet flight to Moi International Airport. Wairimu stepped out of Mzee Ajabu's private jet, holding the day's newspaper, with Kitana and Olivia in tow—all dressed in all black. Olivia had been discharged for the weekend to attend her father's funeral. She could now remember Wairimu and Fred, but everyone else was a stranger to her.

Two journalists and a few of their new corporate friends stepped out, followed by Fred, Jack, and Mrs. Ajabu, whose hand was intertwined with Jamuel's. They stayed behind, whispering and sometimes giggling. Kitana glanced back at them. He did not trust them one bit. And why should he, when they had shown up on the verge of Wairimu's coronation, only to yank the mat from under her feet with the announcement of Mzee Ajabu's death?

In the distance were three dark Toyota Noahs. Wairimu, Kitana, and Olivia got into the first one, their corporate friends and the journalists took the second one, and Mrs. Ajabu and her group dragged their feet to the third one. The cars drove off one by one towards Mzee Ajabu's beach house.

They arrived within the hour. The body had already arrived via Mzee Ajabu's helicopter. Wairimu and Kitana had gone out of their way and used some of Ajabu Digital's profits to make sure Mzee Ajabu's funeral was nothing short of remarkable.

There was a tent provided for the burial ceremony and another tent with a buffet. On the far side of the beach house were well-manicured lawns and pavements leading to a castle-styled marble mausoleum that would not only serve as Mzee Ajabu's final resting place but would also serve as his memorial building.

Kitana was the first one to stand at the podium after everyone was seated.

"I will surely miss him. He was more than a boss to me; he was a father," he said while fighting back tears. "I came to Ajabu Digital when I was a small boy. But he believed in me and held my hand till I could stand on my own two feet and became the man you see here today. May you rest in peace, boss," he said while staring at his casket before taking his seat between Wairimu and Olivia. Everyone clapped except Mrs. Ajabu's group.

"I loved my husband, but God loved him more," Mrs. Ajabu spoke at the podium. "May he rest in peace," she added and went back to her seat as everyone clapped, and her son got up and walked to the podium.

"People who say there is nothing like overnight success are wrong," he began. "Look at me; I'm living proof, and it's all thanks to you, Dad." Fred glanced at his father's casket, and his mother's group clapped as he took his seat.

Wairimu stared at the newspaper on her lap. "MZEE AJABU'S FINAL JOURNEY," the headline read. She averted her gaze from it and looked at her sister. "Olivia, will you say something?" she asked.

Olivia murmured the name Gakenia and started amusing herself with Kitana's tie, her eyes growing wider as if she had never seen one before. Wairimu placed the newspaper on her chair as she stood up and walked to the podium.

She removed her dark sunglasses and wiped her red eyes with a handkerchief before blowing mucus into it.

"I used to resent him," she began after clearing her voice. "But over time, I learned to love him. Like every man, he had his faults. But unlike every man, he has provided the best life he could for us. I will surely miss him. I will miss seeing him coming to the office. I will miss finding him at home, seated next to Mom, enjoying his *ugali* and *sukuma,* and I will miss the feeling of knowing you can mess up because you have a father to fall back onto." Wairimu paused and burst into tears.

Kitana got up and went to her. He supported her and gave her a fresh handkerchief. "I…I know you loved the ocean, Dad," Wairimu stammered. "I hope you find peace here," she added and walked to her seat, supported by Kitana.

A few of their corporate friends gave their speeches, and Jack, Jamuel, Fred, and Kitana carried the casket to the mausoleum.

Next to the crypt were two of Mzee Ajabu's golf kits encased in glass. On top of the glass were his Samsung Note and Kabambe phones.

"I play golf too. We could have gotten along really well," one of the corporate guests said inside the mausoleum before shifting his gaze to the wall.

Mzee Ajabu's favorite clothes were encased in glass frames on the wall, along with the story of how he founded Ajabu Digital, all the accolades his company had won, and full-size photos of him, his three children, and his wife.

"He was quite the man," the guest added.

After the casket was entombed in the crypt, they streamed out of the mausoleum to go to the buffet, except for Wairimu, who remained behind.

"I hope you find peace here, Dad," she stammered in between hiccups. She folded the newspaper that was in her hand in two and placed it on top of the crypt before bursting into tears again.

75.

Diana

When Diana heard Mzee Ajabu was in the hospital suffering from a stroke, she had sold her BMW and covered her Lavington apartment rent, her tennis classes, and her house-help's salary for six months.

He will get well soon, and everything will go back to how it was, she had thought.

The six months had lapsed quickly, together with the half a million shillings that had remained from the sale of her car, and Mzee Ajabu did not seem to be recovering.

Diana got up from her queen bed grumpily and wore her flip-flops like she usually did. She brushed her teeth and had a glass of water before going to the kitchen. Her house-help had prepared an English-style breakfast. She fixed herself a plate and went to the sitting room to eat while watching her favorite show on *E!*.

She switched on the TV and scrolled through her Twitter

feed lazily in between watching her show. She thumbed through the trending topics, and her heart skipped a beat when she saw Mzee Ajabu's name. She thumbed it and froze.

She did not believe it at first; she thought it was a lapse in her memory until she read the headline again. 'MZEE AJABU FINALLY RESTS; THE COUNTRY MOURNS A BUSINESS MOGUL,' it read.

Diana felt dizzy. She looked at the photo of the hearse and felt a headache start to creep up her spine. She stared at the TV for a while without watching the show before she thumbed her mobile money application. Immediately she saw her account balance, she got a full-blown migraine. Only 5,000 Kenya shillings remained from the half a million.

She got up from the couch and went to the kitchen. "Madam, is everything okay?" her house-help was asking her, but she was not hearing. She poured herself a glass of water, swallowed two Mara Moja tablets, and walked slowly to her bedroom. She had a shower, packed her tennis gear into her training bag, and dialed an Uber.

***

"Wait with both hands on your racket on the right side of your body," her middle-aged trainer was saying.

Diana tried to do as she was told. The green ball hit the net and rolled back to her.

"That's a good trial. Let's pick it from the top. This time, don't take your racket back early on the forehand," the trainer shouted from the other side of the court.

Diana dropped the racket and stood still. Another headache was creeping up her spine.

"Diana! Diana!" the trainer called as he walked towards her. "Is everything okay?" he asked with a hand on her shoulder.

"I'm sorry, I have a lot on my mind. Let's take a break today," she said.

"Okay, but if something is on your mind, you can tell me," he said and started to walk away.

"Take a photo of me before you go," she said while running to her training bag and handing him her iPhone.

She was in a red baseball cap, white tank top, red pleated miniskirt, and pink sneakers. *Work or play, always look phresh! #OOTD*, she captioned the photo before posting it on her Instagram profile.

She walked to the changing room while rubbing her temples, had a shower, and changed back into her ripped jeans and Armani knitted sweater, keeping her pink sneakers. She took a photo of her legs. *Pink perfect*, she captioned it and shared it on her Instagram stories.

She took her training bag, walked to a Java, and ordered a vanilla milkshake and a muffin. She took a photo of it immediately the waiter placed it on her table. *Cheat day*, she captioned the photo and shared it on her Instagram stories.

She could now feel her tongue become heavy in her mouth from her headache. She took a sip of her milkshake and a bite from her muffin and felt her stomach become queasy. She paid the bill and dialed an Uber.

They arrived at her apartment, and she realized she did not have enough money to settle the fare. *"Wacha nikulipie leo,"* the Uber driver said. Diana thanked her, got out, and walked sluggishly towards her apartment as her headache turned into a migraine.

76.

Helena

"I HAVE HIS child; this is my house too!"

Helena gripped the iron bars on the gate of Mzee Ajabu's house in Runda as the guard tried to pull her from it by the waist.

"I am not going anywhere until I get my fair share," she groaned. Her lips were cracked, and her clothes hung loosely on her body.

She had downgraded from her Karen villa to an apartment in Madaraka and downsized Helena Beauty Spa to just a salon and moved it to a lower-middle-class neighborhood like her accountant had advised her to. Immediately she did, her high-flying clients had disappeared, together with their money.

The business began registering losses, and Helena had sold her Mercedes S350 like her accountant had advised her and gotten a second-hand Nissan Note. With the sale of the Mercedes came some operational money that would have seen them break even, but it also came with something else: Helena's impatience.

She took huge chunks of money from the business account to buy her friends expensive lunches in the name of business meetings.

"The only way we are going to get back on our feet is by getting our high-flying clients back," she often said, and her accountant would insist that they needed to build brick by brick to get to a place where they could bring back the spa, and then the high-flying clients would follow. But Helena would have none of it, and she soon fired her accountant, after which the business went bust.

"Come to Meadows; we could really use an extra hand with the patients, and you can take time to regroup," her daughter Monica had pleaded with her on the phone.

"I will think about it," she had said.

Instead, she had gone to the bank and gotten a loan with her Nissan Note and what was left of her business as surety. She tried to revive Helena Beauty Spa with the advice her accountant had given her before, but by then it was too late. Her car together with her business were repossessed, and the landlord put a big padlock on the door of her Madaraka apartment.

"I am not going anywhere until I get my fair share," she now groaned, gripping the iron bars on the gate of Mzee Ajabu's Runda home with all her might.

The watchman let go of her and disappeared from the gate. He came back after a while with Mrs. Ajabu in tow. She was in an expensive, flowing, golden gown, her weave touched the small of her back, and in her hand was a large glass of red wine.

"Who are you?" she barked when she got to the gate.

"I am your co-wife," Helena said. "I have Mzee Ajabu's child."

"I have seen you on TV. Aren't you a TV show host or something?" Mrs. Ajabu asked after taking a sip from her wine glass.

"I was. It's just that life happened and..." Helena stammered.

"Is that what TV show hosts do—wreck homes? Mrs. Ajabu said and sipped her wine again as Jamuel joined them, towering and relentless in a white vest, black shorts, and white sandals.

"We were in love. I have his love child," Helena stammered some more. "Please, I haven't paid rent. I haven't eaten all day," she added.

"How are your bastard and your hunger my problem?" Mrs. Ajabu said after sipping her wine. The mention of the word 'love child' had made her boil. "If I ever see you here again, you will join your lover!" she barked, turned around, and headed towards the house.

Jamuel scratched his brown goatee, lifted his white vest, and revealed the pistol that was tucked into his waistband. Helena let go of the gate's iron bars without being asked by anyone and walked away. "We were in love. She is his love child," she said to herself and increased her pace.

77.

Popstar

FRED WAS DRIVEN out of their Runda home at 11:00 am in a black Mercedes G-Wagon that was sandwiched between two gray Toyota Land Cruisers driven by his bodyguards. The ensemble had run the company around 100 million Kenya shillings and depleted the reserve that Wairimu had created. When the CFO raised the alarm, Fred had told him that it was a precautionary measure to protect the company's most prized asset.

He sat in the back-left seat of the G-Wagon and moved his head to the *genge* music that filtered through the speakers. He was in a blue custom-made Armani suit and a Patek Phillipe watch that had run the company another couple of millions.

He got into his breast pocket and came out with a bag of white powder. He poured it on the back of his hand and used a 1,000-shilling note to draw it into a line before closing his left nostril and snorting it with his right. "Now my day has begun," he barked with energy.

When they arrived at Ajabu Digital, one of the bodyguards opened the back-left door, escorted him to his office, and stood guard outside after he entered.

The first thing he did when he sat down on his chair was dial the CFO. "Why am I being paid peanuts?" he barked into the handset. Kitana had reduced his interim CEO salary from three million to 250,000 shillings to try and manage cash flows.

"Kitana…had seen it…prudent to," the CFO stammered.

"Jesus, how long till I'm the laughing stock of the industry? I want it revised to at least 10 million Kenya shillings, with bonuses," Fred barked before hanging up.

He leaned back in his chair, satisfied with his decision, and looked at his Patek Philippe, wondering where Jack and Jamuel were. He was looking forward to his afternoon business deal of buying a music recording company that Jack had said showed promise.

Before he could finish the thought, Jack, Jamuel, and his mother entered his office, accompanied by the music executive. The discussions did not take long before Fred put pen to paper and called his CFO. The business deal was going to set Ajabu Digital back 250 million Kenya shillings.

"It's a steal," Jack said.

"I know, right?" Jamuel echoed his words.

"I'm so proud of you, my son," Mrs. Ajabu beamed.

Fred leaned back in his chair again and grinned. His dream of becoming a celebrated musician was finally taking shape.

78.

Date Night

WAIRIMU SAT ACROSS Kitana in a snug restaurant for dinner. She was in a figure-hugging red dress, silver hoop earrings, red-bottom high heels, and her hair was done in curls. She took a bite from her salmon, then took a napkin and dabbed the grease that was on Kitana's mouth.

"You're welcome," she said with a leery smile.

Kitana smiled. He was in a gray suit and brown leather shoes. He was getting too used to this, he realized.

A breeze wafted through their table, and his scent burned Wairimu's nose. She removed her right shoe and rubbed her foot against Kitana's leg.

"HR will hear about this," Kitana said and smiled again. "Or maybe I should tell my new CEO," he added.

"Has he taken office already?" Wairimu asked while wearing her shoe, her voice somber now and her demeanor sullen.

"Yes, for about a month now," Kitana said while cutting his

steak and forking it. "You should come to the office. You still have a 5% stake in the company, and your father—God rest his soul—named you COO before passing," he added and took a bite.

"I can't stand being around him." She paused. "Does he come alone?" she asked.

"He's usually with your mom and his two favorite henchmen," Kitana said after swallowing his bite. "They are always locked in the office with the Chief Financial Officer. I had instructed him not to let them in on anything, but my words are wind, as you can imagine."

"They are going to destroy in a day what it's taken us months to build," Wairimu said and stared into space.

"You know, Wairimu, I have been thinking about this," Kitana said while placing his knife and fork on the table and straightening up.

"About what?"

"About what happened. It felt planned. It seems to be much more than happenstance."

"What are you saying?"

"I'm saying your father's death might not have been from natural causes."

"Let's just leave it alone," Wairimu said, her eyes turning glassy.

"Let's hire a detective and get to the bottom of it."

"No, Kitana. They have already taken a father from me. Do you want them to take you too, or God forbid, Olivia? Just leave it alone."

"We have worked too hard to leave it alone. Do you want to see us with nothing?"

"Promise me you will leave it alone. Promise?" Wairimu begged, her tears forming tributaries down her cheeks.

Kitana took a napkin and dabbed them away. "Don't cry. I promise," he said unconvincingly.

79.

Detective Rico

HE HAD STARTED as a watchman in a small car wash. He had been a bright student in high school, but his kin could not afford the university fee, and that was how he found himself in Nairobi as a watchman.

His brilliant mind, however, could not allow him to be a watchman for long. He had a knack for sniffing trouble in a way that no one else could.

During the job, his boss's car was hijacked, and he had gone through the trouble of trailing the suspects, only to discover it was an inside job. The car was found and the culprits apprehended, and it was in that way that he was pumped up to chief security of the car wash.

He had used the salary increase to enroll in evening classes in criminology, and before long, he was joining the Kenya Police Force as a corporal. They discovered his talent, and he rose through the ranks and began going on missions around the country to solve cases—from murder to drugs to inheritance. You name it and he solved it.

At the young age of 24, his legend was growing and his reputation preceding him, and that was how he was conscripted into the National Intelligence Unit with a bigger scoop and an even bigger salary.

He had worked there until his retirement age and then decided to start his private practice.

His work was now reduced to contractual. He would be called every now and then by individuals, malls, hospitals, hotels, and corporate offices who wanted investigative work done or their security system reviewed, and that was how he stumbled upon Kitana.

***

RICO NOW SAT at his desk, looking into the eyes of Kitana and remembering the job he had done for Ajabu Digital.

They had a theft problem. By the time he was done, he had not only apprehended the culprits, but also installed a more robust security system of surveillance cameras and keycards that informed senior management who entered and left their offices. After that, theft had become a thing of the past in Ajabu Digital.

"My good friend, how have you been?" Kitana started like all people who need something do.

"You mean I'm your good friend only when it suits you, huh, Kitana?"

"It's not like that. You know how work can be."

"I know how excuses can be." He paused and watched Kitana become uneasy on his chair. "What brings you to this neck of the woods today, friend?" he added and eased the tension.

"A small problem."

"The death of your CEO and the takeover of your company by a drug addict? I would say that is quite the problem," Rico said, his voice reverberating across the room.

"So you have heard the latest on the grapevine?"

"My ear is always on the ground, my friend."

"Will you help a friend out? I don't need to mention that your package would be immense if this turns out to be what I think it is."

"Money?" Detective Rico shrugged. "I always thought you knew me better than that, Kitana."

Kitana glanced at Rico and squirmed in his chair.

"When you get to my age, Kitana, you don't do things because there is money involved. You do them because people you care about will sleep better at night with your help."

"My mistake. Forgive me."

"Don't mention it. How is Wairimu?"

"Stressed," Kitana paused. "A little depressed," he added.

"Send her my regards, and tell her I am taking this job not because of you but because of the man you are becoming by her side."

"I will," Kitana said with gratitude dripping from his words, knowing all too well that the moment Detective Rico accepted the job, it was an open and shut case.

80.

Winery

Mzee Ajabu's helicopter touched down at Naivasha, and Jamuel stepped out in a black shirt, black khakis, and sandals and helped Mrs. Ajabu descend the steps.

Mrs. Ajabu got out in her avocado green romper and adjusted the white halo hat on her head to have a better view of the wine farm she had just purchased for 80 million Kenya shillings.

"Watch your step," Jamuel whispered.

"Thank you," Mrs. Ajabu said as their fingers interlocked, and they started walking towards the winery.

An old man was waiting for them by the building with iron sheets brown from rust and sections of its walls that had completely fallen off. Mrs. Ajabu held onto her halo hat and entered the building.

"Inahitaji kazi kidogo," the old man said.

Mrs. Ajabu jumped over a pool of water on the floor and looked around: The machines seemed to have stopped working

10 years ago, the grape collection bins were full of dirt, and the fermentation barrels were full of holes.

"She's definitely a fixer-upper," Mrs. Ajabu said, underwhelmed.

"We'll fix it." Jamuel pushed his nose into Mrs. Ajabu's neck and breathed. "You won't recognize it once we're done," he added.

"Can I at least sample the wine?" Mrs. Ajabu giggled.

The old man reached on the shelf and dusted off a bottle of red before pouring Mrs. Ajabu a glass. She took a sip and immediately creased her forehead.

"I'm ready to see the vineyard," she said.

They walked into the sun, and she adjusted her hat as they approached the three-acre farm that had torn a hole in Ajabu Digital's cash flows.

"Where are the grapes?" Mrs. Ajabu asked, forgetting herself and taking another sip from her wine. The farm had patches of sun-dried twigs that were moving despondently in the direction of the wind.

"The…grapes?" the old man stammered.

"After we're done with this place, you won't recognize it." Jamuel pushed his nose into Mrs. Ajabu's neck and breathed again.

"You better," she giggled.

Mrs. Ajabu handed the old man her glass of wine and started walking back to the chopper with Jamuel. He had identified another business opportunity—a gym in the heart of Nairobi that would set Ajabu Digital back about 65 million Kenya shillings.

81.

Diana

DIANA WOKE UP from her three-by-six bed exhausted. "I can't go back to the village," she murmured. She had bags under her eyes, and her skin was pale. She turned and sprawled and fell on the floor. She was still getting used to her small bed.

She walked barefoot to the kitchen. There was no breakfast. Her house-help had left the job a month ago, she remembered, and her jaw tensed. She went to open the fridge to get milk for breakfast and remembered she had sold her fridge, together with her cooker too.

She fixed herself a cup of *turungi* and went to the sitting room. Before she sat down, she walked to the shelf to pick her Public Relations class notes. Beside them was the Nairobi Revival Church pamphlet. She picked it together with her class notes and went with them to the sofa.

She stared at the pamphlet for a while before opening her coursework. "I can't go back to the village," she breathed out a sigh while pushing her coursework aside and stared at her TV without switching it on. She had already sold it, and someone was coming to pick it up in the afternoon.

She wondered what she would do with the money. She couldn't continue sinking the little money she was getting from selling her household equipment into paying house bills, she realized.

She sipped her *turungi* and picked her phone. The first text she got was from her tennis trainer. Her classes had been terminated because she had failed to pay. She glanced at the Nairobi Revival pamphlet, clenched her jaw again, scrolled through the app store, and downloaded a tennis game. She played it for a while before opening her Instagram and going through a lingerie store she had been eyeing for a while. "I can't go back to the village," she murmured again and bookmarked some of the garments.

She had not finished drinking her *turungi* when her doorbell rang. It was a messenger with an envelope for her. She took the envelope, sat back on the couch, and removed the letter. She had five days to pay the month's rent or vacate the apartment.

She put the letter back in the envelope and went to have a shower. She dressed in her best clothes and took a mirror selfie. *Small girl with a big God. #Transitions,* she captioned it and posted it on her Instagram profile.

She then sat on the couch and picked the Nairobi Revival pamphlet. She looked at it for a while before picking her phone to continue going through the lingerie store as she waited for the buyer of her TV and later, her sofa, dining set, and some of her designer clothes. She sat and scrolled and waited.

82.

Informant

FRED SNORTED WHITE powder from the breasts of an air hostess who was seated on his lap and stirred with energy. "Now my day has begun," he barked. They were cruising at 40,000 feet in Mzee Ajabu's Gulfstream, headed to Dubai for his music video shoot.

In the cabin were Mrs. Ajabu, Jack, Jamuel, two air hostesses who doubled as Fred's girlfriends, and two of his bodyguards, who sat at the back of the cabin.

"Are the producers ready for us!" Fred shouted amid the loud music that blared in the jet while wiping powder from his nose and pushing the air hostess from his lap. She stood up and buttoned up her blouse before sitting beside him.

"What!" Jack shouted back and gestured to the air hostess to turn down the music.

"Are the producers ready for us?" Fred repeated himself after the music was turned down.

"They better be. They are costing me an arm and a leg,"

Jack said. His gold tooth glinted in the yellow cabin light as he scrolled on his iPad, going through their hotel reservations and video shoot schedule.

"You mean they're costing my company an arm and a leg?" Fred teased, and they all laughed, except for Mrs. Ajabu, who was intertwined with Jamuel on the divan-style seat, gulping wine from a large glass and staring blankly into the distance.

"Mom, is everything okay?" Fred asked.

"Do you think they will ever know what we did?" Mrs. Ajabu said to no one in particular and took a gulp from her glass.

"I called it off a few minutes before they could do it," Fred answered his mother. "What happened down there?" he glanced at Jack.

"I told you. We got there, and he was already gone," Jack replied.

"You mean he finally gave in to the stroke?"

"Either that or someone beat us to it."

"Rest in peace, Dad," Fred said while staring into the distance with a somber face.

"Sometimes, I miss him," Mrs. Ajabu said.

"Don't say such things," Jamuel said while fingering his brown goatee.

"Do you think we did the right thing?" she added.

"What do you mean whether we did the right thing—we did not do anything," Jack said tersely, his gold tooth catching the light and glinting again.

"You have had enough wine," Jamuel said while taking the glass from Mrs. Ajabu's hand.

"Don't take my wine; it's the only thing holding me together," Mrs. Ajabu said, holding on to the glass, but she was no match for Jamuel's strength. He took the glass and summoned the second air hostess to take it to the jet's kitchenette and bring them a glass of water.

Jamuel crushed two sleeping pills and mixed them with the water. "Drink this. It will be good for you," he said while handing Mrs. Ajabu the glass of water. "You're right, Jack. We shouldn't worry about people finding out what we did because we didn't do anything," he added as Mrs. Ajabu took a sip from the glass.

"Our biggest worry should be spending my money," Fred said and the cabin filled with laughter again.

"That's right, Freddie boy," Jack added while gesturing to the air hostess who had brought the glass of water to turn the music back up.

"We shouldn't have done that," Mrs. Ajabu said softly as sleep took her.

Fred grabbed the air hostess that was seated beside him, unbuttoned her blouse, snorted another line of powder from her breasts, and tried to shake off the thought of who else could have wanted his father dead.

83.

Wairimu

WAIRIMU WAS SEATED on the sofa in her Pangani apartment with her phone ringing off the hook.

"Wairimu, I thought our contract involved paying employees and suppliers, not buying guzzlers, ramshackle music labels, wine farms, and gyms?" The CEO of Commercial Bank of Africa barked.

"I'm sorry. My brother and mother are in charge now. My mistake for not telling you earlier. Please terminate the contract before things get out of hand."

"Things have already gotten out of hand, Wairimu, or can you guarantee that the money we have lost will be paid back?"

Wairimu paused, "I…I…I…" she stammered, and the CEO hung up. "Damn it," she cursed and pulled her hair.

She scrolled through her contact list to warn the other stakeholders, but before she could dial a single contact person, her phone went off again.

"I thought we had a 30-day agreement, Wairimu. It's end-month—I have salaries to pay and bills to clear," a supplier complained.

"My brother is in charge. Please take it up with his team."

"I did not sign a contract with your brother; I signed it with you. I trusted you."

"I understand. I'm sorry."

"This is not about understanding and being sorry, Wairimu. You're messing up people's lives. My next move is court," he said and hung up.

She made to thumb her contact list, but before she could, her phone started ringing again. It was a shareholder, then a battery of influencers followed. The tape replayed itself like a broken record every time she picked up.

She couldn't take it anymore. She switched it off, went to the medicine cabinet, and washed down two sleeping pills with a bottle of red wine that was already halfway polished.

"Am I turning into my mother?" she mumbled while lying down on her bed as sleep took her.

84.

Detective Rico

RICO LOCO was what his friends called him because once he put his mind into a case, it drove him crazy until he cracked it.

He started by following Mzee Ajabu's scent, and he came across his lovers. They were both decaying, he realized while watching them from a distance in his surveillance car.

He asked for the CCTV footage of Ajabu Digital's offices and started following Kitana's scent. He saw a diligent man who deserved his success and switched his attention to Wairimu. He watched her ferry newspapers and grow from that to the head of the company, and he felt a great sense of pride.

After he was done with Kitana and Wairimu, he took a trip to Nanyuki, came back, and started following Mrs. Ajabu's scent from way back—to the days of Olivia's abortion. The surveillance camera in the clinic's waiting room told him that the decision was not Olivia's.

The second thing he did was follow her purchasing receipts—they were littered with bottles of wine. *You belong in re-hab,* he thought while looking at the receipts and coming across the rat poison.

Was this the smoking gun he was looking for? He scratched his head. He went through the transactions again and, with a raised eyebrow, looked at the huge amounts of money she had sent to her son, before putting aside her file.

The next thing he did was follow Fred's scent. The scent led him to the doorstep of his drug addiction—a smart boy who was a victim of poor parenting, he thought. But Wairimu was a victim of the same, yet she had turned out differently. He concluded that it was a lack of resolve.

He followed the scent further, into the backyard of Jack and his henchman, Jamuel. They were still running drug rings around the city. He put their photos in his case file. He had a feeling they were connected to this, which was fitting because after the dust settled, he did not plan to leave them on the streets terrorizing good citizens.

After he was done sniffing Fred's scent, he pulled up Mzee Ajabu's hospital files. His clearance allowed him to get a hold of Nairobi Hospital's surveillance cameras, but there was nothing on them. One minute Mzee Ajabu was breathing through a ventilator, then there was a loop that an untrained eye couldn't see, and finally, he lay unmoving. Rico knew that the loop wouldn't hold water as false play in a court of law.

He paced in his office, looking at the pictures pinned on his board: Helena, Diana, Kitana, Wairimu, Olivia, Monica, Mrs. Ajabu, Fred, Jack, and Jamuel. He removed Helena, Diana, Olivia, Monica, Kitana and Wairimu from the board, deciding that they did not have a motive to commit the crime.

He paced across his office again and decided that someone was missing. He looked at the documentation with the doctor's signature that had signed off on Mzee Ajabu's death as a result of a stroke. He looked at the signature closely, realized it resembled the one on Olivia's abortion documents, and decided to pay Dr. Onyango a visit.

85.

Recovering

OLIVIA WOKE UP in the morning, had a shower, and put on her blue uniform. She could now remember everyone except for her mother and their family doctor. She took wet wipes and wiped her baby doll before applying baby powder all over its body and dressing it up in a yellow dress.

"You look lovely, Gakenia," she said before putting it in a baby stroller and walking to the dining hall for breakfast.

She sat down with her banana and mug of porridge—Dr. Karani had observed that the porridge helped increase her appetite. She pinched a chunk of banana and directed it to the doll. "Oh, you're full; that's a good girl." She had not gotten halfway through her breakfast when Monica joined her. They had developed a close friendship in the few months that Olivia had been at Meadows.

"How did your weekend date go?" Olivia giggled into her porridge.

As part of the staff, Monica was allowed to have a social life.

"I don't know about him. He forgot his wallet at home," Monica said, and they both laughed.

She stared at Olivia, still in shock from the news of Mzee Ajabu's passing and even more shocked that Olivia, Fred and Wairimu were her half-siblings.

"What?" Olivia asked with a raised brow.

"What about your Larry?" she tried to recover.

"I don't know about him either," Olivia said while staring into the distance. "He hasn't visited us yet," she said while glancing at her doll. "But he will visit soon, won't he, Gakenia?" she said while extending a hand and tickling the doll.

They finished breakfast, and Monica helped her push the stroller to her psychotherapy session with Dr. Karani while stealing glances from the corner of her eye, trying to spot their resemblance.

Olivia lay on the sofa with the stroller next to her after Monica had left. Dr. Karani opened his notebook and adjusted his weight on his seat across from her. He had observed that the plastic doll helped her cope better with the loss of her child.

"How is your baby?" Dr. Karani asked.

"She's doing good," Olivia beamed.

"I'm glad to hear that," Dr. Karani said while staring at his notebook and reading his notes for a while.

"Can you recall a time when you felt good?" he asked, finally.

"During my dad's 67th birthday," Olivia said.

"What brought the feeling?"

"I wanted to impress him by doing something good for him."

"Did you feel as if you were obligated to impress him?"

"Yes," Olivia said after a while.

"Why did you feel that way?"

"I didn't think he would be accepting of my pregnancy."

Dr. Karani shifted his weight and wrote something in his notebook.

"What feeling do you get when you think about Larry?"

"I feel love, longing, obsession...Sometimes I feel hate."

"What about your mom?" Dr. Karani paused. "And Dr. Onyango," he added.

"I don't remember having a mother," Olivia said after a long pause. "Nor can I remember someone called Dr. Onyango."

***

AFTER LUNCH, MONICA helped her with her duties. She was assigned to clean the windows in the administration block. After they were done, she helped her push her stroller to her hypnotherapy session. She would check back on her after the session for their last activity of the day—a visit to a nearby children's home.

Dr. Karani had seen it fitting for her to start interacting with real kids so that she could begin the acceptance process, and Monica had welcomed it as an opportunity to bond with her further.

Olivia entered Dr. Karani's office and sat down with the stroller beside her after Monica left.

"Focus on the fan on the ceiling and listen to the clinking sounds of this coin hitting my cup," Dr. Karani began. He had tried a couple of ways to hypnotize Olivia: using a pendulum, counting backward from 100, and snapping his fingers. But none of the techniques had worked.

He had gotten the idea of the fan and the clinking sound of a coin on a cup by chance. When his office fan was on, he had noticed a heightened awareness in Olivia. It was when he was getting up to switch it off that a coin had fallen from his shirt pocket into his empty ceramic cup. The effect had made Olivia's eyes roll up, and it was then that he realized he had found her hypnosis trigger.

"I am going to use abstract hypnosis. You will be physically here but psychologically somewhere else," he said like he always did.

Clink, clink, clink. He hit his cup with a coin as Olivia's eyes fixated on the rotating fan on the ceiling and rolled up.

"What feeling do you get when you think about your daughter?"

"Protectiveness and love. She's my rock."

"Do you feel as if you were supported and loved enough while growing up?"

"I don't know," Olivia said.

Dr. Karani shifted his weight in his chair and wrote something in his notebook.

"What comes to your mind when you think about your brother, Fred?"

"Spoiled and obnoxious. But he is also hurting."

"What about your sister, Wairimu?"

"Caring and loving. She also hurts, but she has found a way to be strong."

Dr. Karani wrote in his notebook and wondered what demons Wairimu was fighting. "What about your mom?" he asked, lifting his head. "And Dr. Onyango?" he added.

"Please, please, don't make me remember!" Olivia screamed and came out of her hypnosis.

86.

Detective Rico

DR. ONYANGO'S FILE sat on Detective Rico's desk. It had been delivered to him by a trusted agent who he had partnered with on assignments that crossed borders. Dr. Onyango had resigned from Nairobi Hospital shortly after Mzee Ajabu's death and abandoned his wife and four kids to live lavishly on the island of Santorini with his supermodel girlfriend—with a jet ski and a motorboat in his front yard.

Rico closed his file and shook his head, then glanced at his watch. The clock struck noon. He had a burglary to do.

He found himself in Dr. Onyango's house in Kileleshwa, a little after midday. His wife was at work and his kids in school. He searched the place for evidence with a fine-tooth comb and came up with nothing except the aura of a family without its father— warm but lacking strength. But then again, maybe the house did not need strength, especially when it was coming from a person who could abandon his family for a jet ski and a motorboat.

Rico closed the door behind him, realizing that the trip to Santorini was inevitable, and that was how he found himself on a 13-hour flight to Greece.

***

DETECTIVE RICO AND his contact agent sat down at a café in Fira town for debriefing. The agent had gone through the trouble of tapping Dr. Onyango's phone and installing surveillance cameras in his beach house. He hit play on his recorder, and they listened in.

It seemed money was running short for the doctor. Fred and his consorts had drowned in an alcohol-and-drug-induced stupor and forgotten they had payments to make to their accomplice.

"I have the tape, you know. I will expose you to the press," Dr. Onyango was barking on the call that had gone to voicemail.

It was then that Rico Loco came up with a plan. He would make the good doctor an offer that he couldn't refuse, he thought while leaning back in his chair and grinning.

After a few conversations on an anonymous line, a time and a place were scheduled, and a meeting was arranged.

***

THEY SAT IN a cabana in Oia town while the sun was setting. Dr. Onyango looked weary. He looked to Rico like the kind of man who had never struggled for a day in his life.

Rico had pulled up his file. He was born into a well-off family. Not well-off enough to afford him the lifestyle he wanted but well-off enough to afford him an Ivy-League education and contacts that ensured he got a foot in the door of medicine even when his performance was lackluster. He was a man of shortcuts, Rico realized as thoughts of the illicit private clinic swam in his mind.

Rico adjusted his weight on his chair and looked into Dr. Onyango's bloodshot eyes. He was losing sleep over this, Rico realized. Dr. Onyango pulled out his Ray-Ban sunglasses and put them on, to avoid the heat of Rico's gaze drilling into his eyes.

"Can I see it?" Rico said while clicking a button on his watch and starting the recording. "Five million dollars could set you up nicely." He leaned back in his chair and smiled while running a finger on the black bag that sat beside him.

"I don't know what you're talking about. I don't even know you," Dr. Onyango said in a high-pitched tone.

Rico knew the doctor was playing it safe, which was clever because they had nothing on him as of yet. If they were to wrap up the case, they needed a confession from him or the incriminating tape he said he had or both.

"I understand your fears. I am not a cop or a detective. I am just a supplier that Ajabu Digital screwed over. They owe me upwards of 10 million dollars, so you see, five million is a small price to pay if it means I get my dough back."

"How do I know I can trust you?"

"You don't."

"Then we have nothing to talk about," Dr. Onyango said while standing up.

"I know you need the money, Onyango. The rent on that beach house won't pay itself nor the upkeep for your expensive girlfriend. I think it's time we stopped these cat-and-mouse games. Don't you?"

"How do you know all that?" Dr. Onyango said while sitting back down.

"I do my homework. Ajabu Digital doesn't owe me over 10 million dollars because I'm a fool."

"Okay, okay. I have the tape, but I need the sum wired to my offshore account before we have any further discussions."

Rico removed his laptop from his bag, "What are your details?"

Dr. Onyango gave him his details, and he began tapping on his laptop's keyboard.

"How is Fred? Is he really running his father's company into the ground?" Dr. Onyango asked while breathing hard.

"Fred is a mad dog," Rico said nonchalantly. "And you know what happens to mad dogs. They are put down," he added.

"This whole thing stinks. You know she blackmailed me." Dr. Onyanyo paused for a while. "I should have never gotten involved in this, but life is what it is, isn't it?" he said and looked at Detective Rico for validation.

"You should have gotten a message on your offshore account," Rico said after tapping 'enter' on his laptop's keyboard.

The doctor looked at his phone, and his face gleamed at the sight of the five million dollars. He did not know that that was a shell transaction that wouldn't last 30 seconds. He reached into his pocket and came out with a memory card.

"In that memory card, you will find two *jamaaz* who go by Jack and Jamuel unplugging Mzee Ajabu's ventilator. The two were working in cahoots with Fred and his mother."

"How did you get a hold of this?" Rico asked while inserting the memory card into his laptop and hitting play.

"I was Mzee Ajabu's personal doctor, and I was on duty that day."

"So you turned a blind eye?"

"You could say that. It's not my proudest moment, but life is what it is, isn't it?"

Dr. Onyango's mouth had not closed before Santorini's local police pranced at him. "You are under arrest for the obstruction of justice and as an accessory to the murder of Mzee Ajabu.

Anything you say can and will be used against you in a court of law," one of the policemen said while approaching him with handcuffs.

Dr. Onyango's flight response kicked in. He got up and started running, with the police hot on his heels. He pushed a fruit vendor and ran across the road, almost getting hit by a bus. He jumped over a cliff and fell into a ravine—breaking his neck and dying on the spot.

87.

Music Release Party

FRED WOKE UP in their Mombasa beach house sandwiched between his two girlfriends. The first thing he did was snort powder from both of their breasts. The second thing he did was switch on the TV and play his music video.

"It's a good first trial," one of the girls said.

"This is fucking art," Fred barked.

First CEO popstar, he thought and grinned. Today was a big day for him. It was his music video release party, and he had invited some A-list celebrities that he was looking forward to rubbing shoulders with. Booking them had cost Ajabu Digital an arm and a leg, but it would all be worth it, he told himself as he watched the music video a second time.

He had not gotten halfway through it when his phone buzzed with a message. He looked at it. It was from the Commercial Bank of Africa. They had just terminated their five-year contract with Ajabu Digital. "Screw them," he cursed. "I am going to be a CEO popstar anyway. We will see who has the last laugh," he said to no one in particular and started watching his music video for the third time.

***

THE SUN HAD gone down, and the waters were calm, except for the music that was blaring in Mzee Ajabu's yacht. The invited guests danced, and waiters and waitresses walked up and down the decks with trays of cocktails and bitings as the Sunseeker cruised slowly through the Indian Ocean.

Fred, Mrs. Ajabu, Jack, and Jamuel were in the cocktail bar area of the yacht's sun deck. Mrs. Ajabu was seated next to Jamuel, holding her usual glass of red wine, and Jack was running up and down the decks, coordinating the security and making sure their guests were attended to.

"This is a banger," a guest who had heard about Fred's generosity with money was telling him while moving her hips to the beat.

"Really?"

"Don't forget me when you're famous," she giggled.

"Come, let me show you around."

He took her hand and led her to the yacht's master cabin.

Jack knocked on the door just when he was about to snort a line of powder from her breasts.

"I'm busy," he said irritatedly after opening the door.

"There is a patrol boat on the water. I think they are onto us," Jack said, breathing hard.

"Get lost. We didn't do anything, remember?"

"Could be routine patrols," Jack said. "Or they could be onto us," he added.

Fred closed the door in his face and got back to his guest. He loved his lifestyle, he realized. He did not think for a minute that he needed to do something to sustain it. It also did not cross his mind that his life might have been in danger. It, therefore, came as a surprise when the master cabin's door flew open, and two policemen stood behind it.

"Are you Fred?"

"What…is this…about?" he stammered while jumping out of bed and putting on a shirt and trousers.

"You are under arrest for the murder of your father. You have the right to remain silent…" The words became a blur after he felt cold handcuffs wrapping around his wrists.

"We didn't do it. I called it off," he started pleading as he was escorted out of the main deck of the yacht to find his mom, Jack, and Jamuel being escorted into the patrol boat in handcuffs.

"We shouldn't have done it," Mrs. Ajabu was murmuring.

"Don't say things like that," Jamuel was reprimanding her.

88.

Rebuilding

WAIRIMU STARTED BY demolishing the CEO's and COO's offices and making them part of the talent and training wing. She and Kitana were now left with small cubicles that only fit their desks and a chair.

"I need to operate this company from a position of service, not authority," she told Kitana while placing her favorite teddy bear on his desk. "A gift to remind you about me," she added with a smile.

"What have you decided about Monica?" Kitana asked while cuddling the teddy bear and placing it back on his desk.

"I have decided to let her be," she said while walking out of his cubicle.

The next thing she did was sell the assets her brother and mother had purchased. They all sold for half the price—except for the music recording label, which turned out to be a briefcase company. She used the money to pay a handful of suppliers and influencers.

She rented out their Runda home, deciding that she would continue living in her Pangani apartment. The rent from her childhood home would cater for her upkeep—she had decided she would not take a salary until Ajabu Digital was back on its feet.

After that, she sold her father's private jet and helicopter and closed the branches in Uganda and Rwanda as well as the three floors that Ajabu Digital operated in, so that they now operated on one floor. She sold the office assets to the highest bidder and used all the money acquired from the sale to clear their debts with all their stakeholders.

With Fred facing a life sentence in Kamiti Prison, the company's shareholding was now split between her and Olivia. She thought about Monica for a split second. After Kitana had told her what Rico had discovered, she had called Monica and offered her a position in Ajabu Digital as her assistant, but she had turned down her offer and insisted that her calling was in service.

She averted her thoughts to the company's cash flows. She toyed with the idea of selling part of Olivia's stock and decided against it. In any case, the industry had lost confidence in Ajabu Digital. A handful of clients and employees had left, and more were leaving every day.

"Wherever Tatiana is, she must be having a field day with us," she had joked with Kitana in the lifts.

She recapped the company and spread the shareholding equally between herself, Kitana, Olivia, and their buffer bank. After seeing the changes she had made, Commercial Bank of Africa had agreed to a one-year contract and a buffer of two million Kenya shillings a month to Ajabu Digital. "We will revise the figure as you earn our trust," the CEO had told them.

"We are going to rebuild, brick by brick," Wairimu had said

after they left the meeting.

"We already have a great foundation," Kitana had responded while squeezing her hand.

253

89.

Proposal

WAIRIMU AND KITANA were in Mombasa to complete the sale of Mzee Ajabu's yacht. Wairimu had decided she would keep the beach house and the servants and convert it into a hotel.

When they got to the beach house, the first thing she did was go to her father's mausoleum. She was holding the day's newspaper in her hand. She opened it and glanced at one of the headlines. "MZEE AJABU'S MAGNIFICENT MAUSO-LEUM," it read.

She took a deep breath and moved her gaze to the pictures on the wall. The servants had done a good job maintaining the place: the frames, the photos, and the stories were all intact.

Wairimu stared at her father's photo and felt her eyes become glassy. "I hope you find peace here," she mumbled while wiping them with the back of her hand. She then folded the newspaper in half and placed it on the crypt before getting out of the mausoleum and joining Kitana.

The sun was going down when they met the buyer—a club promoter who wanted to use the yacht for parties. They closed the deal quickly and started walking back to the beach house. She would invest the money from the sale into the talent and training wing and employee bonuses, Wairimu thought. She moved to hold Kitana's hand, but he pulled away.

She glanced at him. He had been acting strange all day, and she was starting to wonder if, like most of Ajabu Digital's stakeholders, he was also thinking of leaving.

They got into the beach house, and one of the servants directed them towards the backyard, where their dinner had been set up with the backdrop of the Indian Ocean. Wairimu's jaw dropped when she saw the setup: There were petals of red roses scattered along the walkway to the candle-lit table, beside which a fire crackled and two other servants waited for them.

"What is this all about?" Wairimu asked nervously as Kitana pulled a chair for her, and a servant gave them hot towels to clean their hands before pouring them a glass of wine each.

"A small way to appreciate all your hard work," Kitana said while sitting across from her.

"It was a team effort," Wairimu said, embarrassed. "In any case, I should be the one thanking you for Detective Rico," she added, her cheeks flushing red as she opened the first hotpot.

It had pan-fried prawns. She closed it and opened the second one. It had oysters. She opened the third hotpot and stared at it, speechless. It had an 18-carat diamond ring. She lifted her gaze to look at Kitana. He was down on one knee.

"Working alongside you has been an honor; being your boyfriend has been the best thing that happened in my life. Wairimu Ajabu, will you make me the happiest man on earth by giving me the pleasure of becoming your husband?"

"Yes," Wairimu said without a second thought.

Kitana took the ring and pushed it up her ring finger as the servants clapped, the fire crackled, and the waves on the Indian Ocean broke.

90.

Smoking Gun

DETECTIVE RICO SAT in his office with a bad taste in his mouth. He bit into his apple, leaned back in his chair, and the feeling that he had been fooled erupted in his gut. He went to his board and stared at the names that were there before opening his laptop and playing the CCTV clip that Dr. Onyango had given him.

He saw Jack and Jamuel enter Mzee Ajabu's room wearing doctors' garb; Jamuel stood as the second pair of eyes at the door as Jack took a phone call. He put the phone in his pocket and stared at Mzee Ajabu for a while before unplugging the ventilator and then securing it back again.

He rewound the clip and zoomed in. The cardiac monitor was already registering a single line before Jamuel and Jack entered the room, he realized. He bit into his apple and thought for a while before leaning towards his laptop and replaying the clip.

Just as the clip started, a nurse in baggy scrubs folded a newspaper in half and placed it next to Mzee Ajabu before leaving the room.

Her movements were such that her body obscured the cardiac monitor, and her face was covered with a surgical mask and a hairnet. Less than a minute later, the door opened, and Jack and Jamuel entered the room.

Rico took his phone, dialed the security team of Nairobi Hospital, and asked for the surveillance footage of the parking lot on the day Mzee Ajabu's death was registered. Within a few minutes, his email pinged with a message. He downloaded the clip and began going through it with a fine-tooth-comb.

He watched Jack and Jamuel drive into the parking lot in a Porsche Cayenne. Immediately they did, the door of a gray Volkswagen Golf flew open across from them, and a nurse in baggy scrubs, a surgical mask, and a green hairnet got out of the driver's seat while holding a newspaper with hands covered in surgical gloves.

Rico leaned back in his seat and took a bite from his apple while re-watching the beginning of the clip. He watched the nurse fold the newspaper and place it next to Mzee Ajabu, again and again, in slow motion. In between pauses, he realized he had seen Wairimu do the same exact thing in the Ajabu Digital CCTV footage of her days ferrying newspapers as an intern.

He leaned back and gasped. He made to take a bite from his apple, but he had finished it. He picked up his phone and dialed Kitana's fiancé with the same bad taste in his mouth.

91.

Visiting Day

WAIRIMU PUSHED OLIVIA'S stroller as they walked together towards the field. She was in a bright red jumpsuit and black sandals. "Where is Monica?" she asked as they stopped at a green patch of grass.

"She's volunteering at a nearby children's home," Olivia replied.

"Tell her to join us next time," Wairimu said. She removed her sandals, got into her *kiondoo,* and laid down a *leso.* As they sat down, she placed the day's newspaper on the *leso.*

"I will. She's great company, and she's been like a sister to me," Olivia said, picking the newspaper and going through the pages. "AJABU DIGITAL REBUILDING UNDER THE GUIDANCE OF ITS BOSS LADY," the headline on one of them read, with a full-length photo of Wairimu standing in true boss-lady fashion.

"Congratulations, sis," Olivia beamed.

"I need you to get well so you can help me get it back to where it was," Wairimu said while getting into her *kiondoo* and coming out with a box of pizza and a bottle of Fanta Orange.

"I will try. That is, if you don't make me so fat that I can't even walk," Olivia said while tucking a strand of hair behind her ear, opening the box, and picking up a slice of pizza.

"You have great genes, sis," Wairimu chuckled, surprised by how quickly her sister was recovering. "You could eat pizza every day and never lose that figure," she added, and they both laughed as she removed two cups from the *kiondoo* and unscrewed the cap on the bottle of Fanta Orange.

"How is Dad?" Olivia asked while biting her pizza.

"He's still in critical condition," Wairimu said, impressed that Olivia's first instinct was to eat the pizza instead of trying to feed it to her plastic doll as she usually did. "I'm crossing my fingers, but whatever happens, know that we have each other," she added while filling up Olivia's cup with Fanta.

"I hope he pulls through. I miss him," she said after taking a sip from her cup. "What about Fred?" she asked.

"You know Fred is Fred," Wairimu replied while taking a sip from her cup, and they both laughed. "I have great news, though," she said while putting her cup down. "I'm getting married."

"You're getting married?" Olivia said with wide eyes. "Congratulations!" She dropped her slice of pizza into the box and attacked Wairimu with a hug. "Who is the lucky guy?" she asked.

"Kitana, our COO. I don't know if you remember him?"

Olivia stared into the distance for a while. "It doesn't matter. I am super excited for you," she said, attacking her with another hug. "It will be just as beautiful as mine and Larry's was," she added.

"I hope it is," Wairimu said. Dr. Karani had told her that

sometimes recovery began by reinforcing the memories—real or imagined—that made the patient feel good about themselves.

When is the wedding? I have to be your bridesmaid," she beamed.

"I will give you all the deets," Wairimu giggled.

They finished their pizza and soda and then got up and threw the empty bottle and box in a nearby bin. Wairimu folded her *leso* and put it into her *kiondoo* handbag. She wore her sandals, picked the newspaper, folded it in half, and they started walking towards the administration block.

Wairimu glanced at Olivia and noticed in delight that she had forgotten her stroller behind. It was only a matter of time before she recovered completely. It was only a matter of time before she got her sister and her chief of staff back, she thought.

She had not finished her train of thought when her phone started ringing. She glanced at it; it was Detective Rico. Her heart skipped a beat before she thumbed the green receiver button. She replied with mmh's and uh's before thumbing the red receiver button and staring into the distance as they walked.

"Who was it?" Olivia asked.

"It was Kitana," Wairimu replied evenly.

"Tell him I said hello," she said excitedly.

"I will," Wairimu said with a distracted tone. She glanced at the newspaper she was holding, and the conversation she had had with Detective Rico ran across her mind again. He was inviting her to his office for a cup of coffee, but she sensed it was more than that. If he had figured it out, Ajabu Digital and Olivia would be in good hands with Kitana, she knew.

Epilogue

It was a Friday evening. Diana and Helena were in Nairobi Revival Church for the evening service and choir practice ahead of the church's Sunday service. Diana was in a long frock and a baggy sweater, and Helena was in a puffy jacket and trousers. They glanced at each other and smiled.

They had been ecstatic when they met each other again. Helena saw her daughter in Diana—she could be a mother to her in a way she had never been to Monica, she had thought. Diana had seen the cool mom she had never had.

Their stories about Mzee Ajabu had only bonded them further. They glanced at each other again and smiled.

Diana removed her phone and took a selfie. *Soul Food,* she captioned the photo and posted it on her Instagram profile as they opened their hymn books and started choir practice.

After choir practice, they got in line to serve tea and *mandazi* while waiting for the service to begin.

"You have a very beautiful voice," a young gentleman said while turning his gaze to look at Diana.

"Thank you," she said and blushed.

"I have been seeing you around a lot lately. How long have you two been at Nairobi Revival?" An older gentleman was turning his gaze to look at them.

"Not long," Helena said. "We're new in town," she added.

"Oh, we could show you around," the younger gentleman said.

"Wait, let me see if they have any rings on their fingers," the older gentleman said while picking Helena and Diana's hands to inspect them. "All clear," he said, and they laughed as they shared their contact details.

The younger and older gentleman high-fived as they walked to their seats with their tea and *mandazi*.

After the service, Diana and Helena found themselves at a pub having *nyama choma* and a few beers. They glanced at the TV in the pub that was switched to news. "MOTHER AND SON LAWSUIT FOR A SLICE OF AJABU DIGITAL DISMISSED," the headline read. They gave each other knowing looks and started whispering and giggling.

The hour hand was at midnight when they finished their supper and entered the pub's restrooms. Helena changed out of her puffy jacket and trousers into a figure-hugging red dress that cut below her hips and sank her feet in black high heels. Diana changed out of her long frock and sweater into a pink skater dress and brown wedge heels.

They looked into the mirror and did their makeup with heavy mascara and red lipstick before picking their purses and stepping out onto the road that was dimly lit by a few working street lights.

A Toyota Probox slowed down next to them after a few

minutes on the road and drove off after a while. A Toyota Vitz followed and drove off. A Porsche Cayenne slowed down and stopped. Diana and Helena got in, and it drove off for the second part of their service.

If You Enjoyed This...

If you enjoyed The Sponsor, take one minute to spread the word in the form of a short review on your social sites or a whisper to a friend or two. I will be thankful and new readers will be too.

K. Kimuyu

DRUG PARADISE

They know everything about you,
you know nothing about them,
they are coming for you.

Turn page to read preview...

The Couple

"You know what to do when you get to Nairobi, don't you, hon?" Lily said. She was better known by her alias, Quicksilver. Like mercury, she moved liquidly and changed unpredictably.

She circled her fiancé as if she were a vulture and he were carrion while straightening his collar and tying his tie, the scent of her L'Oreal hairspray mixed with her Dior perfume burning his nostrils. That was the difference between her and Marion: Marion was elegant but simple. Lily was in your face with a rambunctious style.

"There are about ten kilos of juice in that briefcase," she said.

Juice was the name they had given to cocaine.

"Make sure it gets to Frankie, he's our distributor in Nairobi. You're taking a private jet from Tom Mboya International Airport to Wilson Airport."

"You won't use the main entrance. You know our contact

person there, don't you? He will direct you to a safe entry and our pilot will be waiting for you. Do you want me to run over it again?" she whispered, her breath misting his ear.

"Do you want a bit of something to get you focused?" She stretched her leg out of the flimsy, silk lace cloth that looked like an expensive leso, grabbed Oyunga's hand, and directed it up her inner thighs pushing up one of his fingers inside her and letting out a savage moan. "I won't take long, I promise." Oyunga pushed his finger further up, brushing against brittle pubic hairs and parting her inner lips. Lily let out a rabid groan of approval.

He got up, pushed her against the wall, and undid the knot tying the lace cloth around her waist, yanking it off her forcefully to reveal plump buttocks. Lily arched her back, the dip on the small of her back and the rise of her hips resembling a valley, and her legs split apart out of habit.

He plunged in and out of her and as she let out trumpeted moans, he wondered if his aggression was raw desire or if he was trying to prove that he was the man. A man who was in charge, a man who didn't need his fiancée in his ear repeating a brief to him over and over again as if he were a little boy.

Small Argument

SHE STOOD THERE STICKY, the wetness still on her.

"Daddy."

A coarse sound escaped her amid heavy breathing after they were done. She bit her lower lip and watched her fiancé walk to one of the shelves and pick up a pistol. The Browning Hi-Power. He loved its wooden handle and the grip it provided but even more than that, he loved how light and smooth it was.

He removed the cartridge. There were thirteen rounds in the chamber. Oyunga put the pistol back together, wondering how he had gotten into the deep end of all of it. He had a successful career as a chef, yet here he was reassembling a semi-automatic handgun.

"I told you, you don't need a gun. Our friend has provided you with a bodyguard."

They used the name 'friend,' when referring to people in positions of power in government. Governors, senators, judges, army generals. The upper echelon was all in on it.

"How many times will I tell you I don't need a bodyguard?"

"It's for your own safety, hon." Her face had now turned from a face that was dripping with pleasure to one that was full of concern. "Anything can happen out there. We're not selling bread and bananas to a kiosk. This is juice. This is life and death."

"What tells you I don't understand that?" he asked while tucking the Browning Hi-Power into his waistband and covering it with his cobalt blue blazer. "I will be back on Sunday evening. You can wait for me at the airport but I'd prefer it if you didn't. I don't want to trouble you. I'd rather you were here bathing in bath salts, prettying yourself up for me."

"Ten million shillings is not little money, hon. Plus I'm a woman, I can multitask between picking you up at the airport and prettying myself up with bath salts, don't you agree?"

He knew that if she had her way she would be accompanying him to Nairobi. She was the kind of person who wanted to micromanage everything but he had a feeling that she had more pressing business in Mombasa that she didn't want to let on. He picked up the briefcase that had the juice and kissed her on the forehead.

"See you Sunday."